**SHE WAS TIMELESSLY BEAUTIFUL.
SHE WAS ALSO THE OLDEST
HUMAN ALIVE.**

Now all the pieces fell together. Lilith was an emortal; Alex Germain no longer had any reason to doubt her.

"So you were one of the first," he said to her. "You're a Cro-Magnon."

"That's right," said Lilith.

"Something like 25,000 years old . . . you must be a little tired."

She looked at him emptily. "I was tired before they built the first pyramid along the banks of the Nile, before they molded the first adobe bricks for the tower of Babel.

"But I have the curse of life."

A MESSAGE TO THE READER

Before his death in 1983 after a long illness, Mack Reynolds had taken several novels to first-draft stage and then, perhaps driven by a sense of mortal urgency, gone on to the next. When it became clear that Mack would be unable to bring them to completion, I, with Mack's and later his estate's approval, commissioned Dean Ing to take the entire group to a fully polished state. Dean's purpose has not been to collaborate posthumously, but to finish them exactly as Mack Reynolds writing at the utter top of his form would have done.

We believe that Dean has succeeded to an almost uncanny degree. For any writer, and particularly one of Ing's stature, to so subordinate his own authorial personality is a remarkable achievement.

Requiescat in pacem, Mack.

—Jim Baen

I liked Mack; I liked the way he lived; and I liked his tequila. That's why . . .

—Dean Ing

In my opinion, we can achieve at least partial success in extending the human life span by the year 2000 . . . By the year 2025, it could be possible for us to gain complete control over the aging process and to develop highly advanced methods of rejuvenation and repair of aging, disease and accident victims . . . And by the middle of the twenty-first century, we could well become true immortals—genetically reprogrammed to live on indefinitely, instead of growing old and dying.

> —Saul Kent
> *The Life Extension Revolution*

Aging and death are not inevitable . . . Aging, being so gradual, presumably depends on very minor biochemical changes, which, once known, may be treatable . . . I believe that, once the mechanism is known, a treatment to stop aging completely may soon be found, possibly before 2000 . . .

> —Desmond King-Hele
> Fellow of the Royal Society

If you can hang on until the year 2000 you can probably name your own life span.

> —Arthur C. Clarke
> In a conversation with the author

Eternity . . . Eternity,
Where will you spend . . . Eternity?
—Old Hymn

Chapter 1

1.

The girl he had met on a bench in the plaza near the bus stop had told him the only hotel in town suitable for a gringo was the Casa de Sierra Nevada. He had been somewhat amused by her vehemence about the Spanish Colonial town of San Raphael de Aldama. It was, she assured him, grim, drab, uninteresting and with nothing whatsoever for a traveler to enjoy. In fact, it was the deadest town in Mexico.

She had elaborated on the fact to considerable end, and as he listened it came to him where he thought he had seen her before. She was the spitting image of Queen Nefertiti, wife of Pharaoh Amenhotep IV. He had seen the famous bust in the Egyptian Museum, opposite Schloss Charlottenburg in West Berlin.

What had been her name? Lilith . . . Lilith Eden and had she bothered to use cosmetics and an attractive hair-do and to have attired herself in something more winsome than slacks, sweater and leather sandals without socks, she would have been a knockout.

Lilith had been correct, there was little to indicate that Calle Hospicio Number 15 was a hotel. There was a discreet little sign in colored tile set into the wall to one side of the doorway announcing that it was the Posada de Sierra Nevada but the proprietors hadn't seemed to find it necessary to add that it was a hotel, pension, inn, or whatever.

One half of the massive double wooden door was hospitably open and he entered into a domed stone *entrada* that stretched perhaps twenty feet before debouching into as beautiful a patio as he could off-hand remember having seen. His eye immediately caught bougainvillea vines in several colors, fuschias, elephant ears, succulents, geraniums and even orchids. He had forgotten that orchids prospered at this altitude in Mexico. San Raphael was over a mile high, which accounted for its near-perfect climate. Though in the tropics, the altitude and semi-arid countryside defeated both heat and humidity.

He put down his bags and looked around. Three doors, spaced out, gave entry into what was seemingly a diningroom to the left. To the far end, the door was obviously for serving and opposite it, across a short corridor, the establishment's kitchens. On the other side of the patio were three more doors, the one nearest the street with a discreet sign that announced "Bar". The one next to the kitchen looked as though it led into the hotel office and he headed for it. The whole establishment had undoubtedly originally been one of the Spanish

Colonial mansions he had been passing on his way. To the right of the office door was a small fountain built into the wall, a stone frog delivering a stream of water into the basin below it. Alex decided that the frog must have been young not more recently than a couple of centuries ago.

Alex headed for the office just as its screen door opened and a striking woman issued forth briskly, a small sheaf of papers in hand.

Alex Germain stared at her. Her tall, shapely figure was in velveteen black slacks and a fluffy white silk blouse. She was a blonde, animated of face, obviously business-like with a vengeance. She seemed to be in her early forties but projected the vivaciousness of a decade or more younger. She wore but one piece of jewelry, a single gold earring of several loops. That came back to him. So did the rest of her, for that matter, but especially the single earring.

"Nuscha!" he said.

She came to an abrupt halt and took him in. "The name is Ursula Zavala," she said stiffly. She frowned, obviously wanting to know just who he was.

He grinned at her. "There's not a girl in Austria named Ursula who isn't called Nuscha as a diminutive. Nuscha . . . uh, Richter. You used to run that pension-bar on, let me remember, Maria Theresien Strasse, just across the Universitats Strasse from the university in Vienna. Holy smog, it must have been twenty years ago. If you hadn't wanted me to remember, we should never have killed that night together, beginning in the Rathaus Keller."

She took him in again, on the face of it quite honestly not remembering at all. She said slowly, shaking her head, "My name used to be Ursula Richter, and I used to manage the Theresien Pension, but I am afraid . . ."

He laughed, as though forgivingly, "I was only there for a week or so. Covering some scientific symposium or other. Quite a few of the older professors hung out at your place, so that's where I stayed."

She shook her head again, regretfully. "I'm afraid that when you're in the hotel business a good many people come and go. You must have been very young at that time." She took in the bag and typewriter that he'd put down on the other end of the patio. "Were you looking for accommodations?"

"I don't have a reservation," he told her. "I hope you have room. Lilith Eden told me this was the only place possible to stay in San Raphael."

"Oh, don't worry about that," she sighed. "Sometimes I feel like a hermit. This town isn't exactly crawling with visitors. My husband must have been insane to have bought the Sierra Nevada. If you'll bring your things . . . I'm afraid the boys are all tied up for the lunch hour." She tossed her papers to a small patio table.

He went back and got his suitcase and typer and rejoined her. She led the way into the same door that he'd seen a waiter enter earlier. They emerged into a serving room, centered by a table that was tastefully covered with desserts, fruit, and a large cheeseboard. Beyond, to the left, he could see into the establishment's dining rooms, two of them in a row. The first would have seated perhaps thirty-five and the smaller room beyond, with but one circular table, only six. There were possibly twenty persons at lunch and three of the nattily dressed waiters seeing to their needs. The clientele was elderly. She turned to the right, passed two rest-room doors and then led the way up a narrow staircase. The steps were of stone and well worn with what must have been several centuries of use.

"What was your name?" she said, over her shoulder.

"Alex. Alex Germain."

"What in the world are you doing in this part of Mexico? We don't see many tourists."

"Holiday. Trying to seek out some of the backwater spots nobody's ever heard of. Vague idea of gathering material for an article. Mexico's been done so much, you'd need a really new angle."

"Oh, that's right. You're an author. You said you were covering some scientific thing in Vienna."

"Writer," he said dryly. "Authors produce literature. Freelancers churn out commercial copy for the magazines. I have no delusions of grandeur."

At the head of the stairs was a door. She opened up, not needing a key, and ushered him into a room the side of a dormitory.

He was flabbergasted. The nearest thing he had ever seen to it was in the Spanish government posada in Granada that had been converted from a palace which had once housed Queen Isobel herself.

He shook his head even as he put his luggage down, and looked about. The furniture was heavy, Spanish Colonial in style, and looking like real antiques. There was even a canopy over the monstrously large bed. While she stood there in the room's center, looking somewhat amused, he went about on an inspection tour. The tile bathroom was larger than many a room he had occupied in swank hotels throughout various parts of the world. There was not only a fireplace in the livingroom cum bedroom, but a smaller one in the bath as well.

He went over to a set of French windows, pushed them open and stepped out onto a terrace large enough that he could have thrown a party for forty people. The terrace looked out over San Raphael giving an excellent view of the center of town, with the pink spires of La Parroquia dominating. There was comfortable looking porch furniture.

He went back into the room and said to her dryly, "What is this, the royal suite?"

She said, "I have only six suites. This is the smallest. You mentioned delusions of grandeur when it came to being a writer. My husband had them pertaining to being a Boniface."

Alex let air from his lungs. "What's the tariff?"

"A thousand pesos a night."

He looked at her. "Are you trying to make all your money from one customer? I can stay in Acapulco for less than that."

She nodded. "I know. But the thing is, I have a monopoly in San Raphael. And, to get by, I need it. I get so few guests that I've really got to charge them or I can't hack it."

"You must absolutely run people out of town," he said ruefully.

"There's a little Mexican fonda, a block off the Zócalo. They only charge two hundred."

"With bath?"

"They've got a toilet, shared by all the rooms. There's a lavatory in it."

"And me without a bath for three days. No thanks. I'll stay here. Your dining room also looks tempting. And you've even got a bar. Listen, I'm going to have a shower and get into something clean. But how about having a drink with me in about fifteen minutes? Along with tacos to eat, warm beer is all I've had to drink for what feels like thousand of miles."

She smiled and shot a glance at her watch. "The dining room doesn't seem to be particularly busy. I should be able to squeeze it in. Listen, did you used to wear a beard when you were staying at my pension in Vienna?"

"I think so," he said, remembering. "They wore beards in those days. I was probably trying to look older."

She was scowling at him. "But I thought you were British. I seem to remember you with an Oxford accent."

He laughed. "I say," he clipped out. "My dear old Mater in Ohio would never forgive you, don't you know?"

"That night we killed, as you put it, is beginning to come back to me. But I'm sure I remember a British accent."

"Probably an affectation I was putting on. You know how kids are."

She turned to go.

He said, "Do I get a key?"

She looked back at him. "Oh, sorry, there are no keys. But you don't have to worry. This isn't the

States. There hasn't been a crime in San Raphael since they lynched the local priest during the revolution. And don't ask me to put some valuable in the hotel safe. We don't have a safe."

2.

He entered the Sierra Nevada Bar just about on time, that is, fifteen minutes later. Ursula Zavala hadn't made her appearance as yet. He was feeling wonderful after a prolonged shower and after a complete change in garb ranging from socks to fresh slacks and a clean sport shirt. Although some of the older types he had seen in passing in the dining room wore suits and ties, he assumed that informality was acceptable in a town like San Raphael. It would have to be so far as he was concerned. He had a light jacket in his things but that was as much as he could mount when it came to sartorial elegance.

The bar was more of a lounge than a classical saloon. There were no facilities, at the bar proper, to sit or even to stand, to take one's drink. The decor was attuned to the balance of the Sierra Nevada. Very elegant, indeed. There was even a piano at the far end of the room. The seating arrangement was largely ultra-comfortable looking sofas and well upholstered chairs with cocktail tables strategically spaced about. It would have accommodated possibly forty but at this time of day there were only half a dozen patrons, two, obviously man and wife, were in their early middle years and somehow looked out of place. The others were all men, the youngest possibly going on sixty.

The room was well done. A large fireplace, at present cold, at one end of the rectangular room. Wall to wall carpeting in battleship gray. The walls were in some twenty-five very old looking prints of ships and sea charts of yesteryear. All very well done indeed.

The bartender left his post and came over.

"¿Si, señor?" he said.

He was young, neat, and attired as the waiters in the dining room. Alex could see that Ursula had brought Teutonic institutions to Old Mexico. The fellow's shirt was even clean.

"If I drink any more tequila, I'll turn into a maguey plant," Alex said. "¿Tiente usted cognac Frances?"

"Of course, señor," the other smiled with a touch of un-waiter-like condescension. "Any particular brand, sir?"

So Ursula even had her boys speaking English.

Alex said, "VSOP Martell?"

"¿Porque no?" the other said and returned to his station for the order. Now that the newcomer noticed, there was a wide selection of potables at the bar, wide enough so that most of them must have been imports. Mexico didn't produce such a variety.

As Alex had entered, he had passed a small table near the door that had a pile of magazines and newspapers on it. On the top had been a copy of the *Journal of the American Gerontology Society*, along with such publications as *Time-Newsweek* and sections of *The New York Times*. He was about to get up to find himself something readable when Ursula Richter—no, it was Zavala now—

entered and smiled at him. She looked a little on the harried side.

She came over and said, "Sorry I'm late ... Alex." She called out greetings, or made with a wave of her hand, to the others present, all of whom seemed to know her. He got the quick impression that the owner of the Sierra Nevada was not only well known but popular. But then she would be if she managed the only decent place in town to eat and drink. And if she was anything at all like the Nuscha he had known of old.

She plopped herself down on the sofa beside him.

"I just got here," he said. "That's one king-size bathroom you supplied me with. Wonderful. Two drinks, well, I can be broken down, maybe three, and then I'm going to hit that dining room. Have you got a decent chef?"

"Ought to be," she sighed. "I'm it."

"You mean you're the cook as well as everything else?"

"That I am."

The barman came up with a tray and put a glass of white wine before his employer and a snifter glass of brandy before Alex, as well as a tab.

"Gracias, Paco," Nuscha said as she was served.

Alex gratefully took up the drink, his eyes inadvertently taking in the chit as he did so.

He looked at his companion. "Eighty pesos!" he said in protest. "For one drink? You must drive customers out like lemmings."

She shrugged. "Mexican taxes on imported luxuries are horrendous. You should stick to tequila, or locally distilled rum."

He gave up. "I suppose you're got a monopoly, so nobody can boycott you. But I thought one of the reasons people came down to Mexico was for the cheap prices." Something came to him and he added absently, "As a matter of fact I was thinking of buying a little place to use as a base of operations. You know, a small house I could leave my books and things in and come down several months out of the year. Possibly rent it out when I wasn't in residence."

She said, a bit hurriedly he thought, "Oh, you wouldn't want to pick San Raphael."

"Why not?"

"Well, it's very dull for one thing. Nothing to do."

"That's what Lilith Eden said," Alex told her. "If it's as boring as all that, why do you hang on?"

Ursula shrugged and made a moue. "It's all Eduardo left me," she said. "If I could sell out, I would. But who'd buy a white elephant like this? As it is, it's more or less of a living."

"Who makes up your guests?"

She shrugged that off too. "Oh, there's enough of a foreign colony, mostly elderly retirees, to support one small establishment. The rooms rent out to occasional travelers such as yourself, or to friends or relatives of the local colony who come to visit."

"So it's pretty dull, eh?"

She snorted. "Sometimes I feel like breaking my arm, just to hear the bone snap."

He laughed. "You know, you neither look nor act any older than I remember you. It's just come to me that at least twenty years have passed."

She took a sip of her wine and nodded. "As they say, flattery will get you everywhere."

"No, I mean it."

She said, "I should have listened to my first cosmetic surgeon. He told me, quite frankly, that it was a battle I couldn't win. I was sleeping with him so I should have known he was being honest."

"How do you mean?"

She sighed and ran a hand down over her smooth cheek. "With face lifts you have the first one, a little nip here, a little tuck there, and, behold, you're looking twenty years younger. But five years later you need another. And three years later, another. And then you're hooked and they become necessary every year or so. If you stop, bingo, within a few months you've taken on the wrinkles of several normal decades. All of a sudden in appearance you're a grandmother."

She sighed and ran the hand down over her face again, this time touching the laugh wrinkles at the side of her startlingly blue eyes. "I suppose I've reached the point where I'm going to have to call the battle quits. There's no reason why not. Since my husband died, I've no particular reason to continue trying to look as though I'm still a young woman."

She switched the subject, as though uncomfortable with it. "You know, I still can't pinpoint our meeting in Vienna. Who were you working for?"

"I think that assignment was for the *London Illustrated News*. A scientific gabfest."

"*London Illustrated News*? You mean to tell me that long ago you were writing for them and, since then, you haven't advanced beyond the point of writing things for second rate magazines?"

He took another sip of the aged brandy. "That's the way the pickle squirts. Oh, I've had some newspaper jobs from time to time but I'm not cut out for discipline, I suppose."

One of the waiters came in and said, "Teléphono, Señora."

She finished her wine and came to her feet. "A hotel manager's work is never done," she said. "You'll be eating here?"

"In moments," he told her. "I'm starved."

"I'll tell Marcelo to ready a table for you."

When she was gone, he looked down at the few drops of his remaining cognac and wondered whether to order another. It came to him that Nuscha's face didn't show any of the very faint scars one usually associates with face lifts, up near the temples, along the neck line. If he'd followed Ursula Zavala correctly, she claimed to have had at least several.

The married couple he'd noted upon his entrance to the bar were seated, in a couple of armchairs, only a few feet away.

The man said, "Couldn't help overhearing you. Didn't you say you might be looking for a house to buy in San Raphael?"

Alex looked over at them. Rather typical Americans. Dressed possibly a bit more stuffily than was called for in travelers. The man wore a rather loud tie and the woman had a dowdy dress of the type the British call a frock. From the voice, the man, at least, was probably a Texan. Southeastern Texas. San Antonio? They were drinking mixed drinks, probably Margaritas by the look of the salt on the glass rims.

"Might be," Alex said. "Just keeping my eye open as I travel around."

"Forget about it," the other said in disgust. "There are no houses for sale in this dog-goned town."

Alex looked at him. "How do you mean?"

"Mother and I've been looking for nigh onto a week now. When we first spotted this here town, we thought we found what we'd been looking for. You know, pretty atmosphere, like. Top notch climate. Looks like it oughta be cheap too."

Alex waved to Paco, the bartender, for a refill.

He said, "The foreign colony I've seen all seem to be on the older side. There ought to be quite a few vacancies as retired people pass away."

The woman said, her voice even more southern than that of her spouse, "You'd think so, but there's not."

"Isn't there a real estate dealer?" Alex said.

"He'd starve to death," the man told him in disgust.

"I'd think Mrs. Zavala could help. She'd be up on all the San Raphael news."

"She's been mighty nice," the other grumbled. "But she didn't come up with any houses. Not even for rent. We figured we might rent a house and stick around six months or so until something opened up. But we couldn't even locate a decent rental." He snorted. "Decent, hell. We couldn't find nothing period."

The bartender came with a fresh glass of brandy and Alex took it up. "You know," he said. "What you might consider doing is buying one of the ruins. As I came into town on the bus, it looked to me as though about a third of the old houses were practically falling down. I'd think these poorer Mexicans living in them would be glad to sell for a reasonable amount. Then it'd be up to you to rebuild. Put in electricity, plumbing . . ."

He at the neighboring table looked at him in just short of contempt for that opinion. "That occurred to us the first week. But those houses in ruins are mostly lived in by squatters. They don't own them at all. And when you try to find out who does own 'em, you run into a brick wall."

"Do you speak Spanish?"

"Enough to get by. Mother and me been living around Chicanos all our life. But that wasn't it. Even when we did find out who owned some likely place, we weren't able to make contact. We've just about given up."

The woman said, a touch of indignation there, "But that's not all. They're not friendly here. We been here a long time and nobody hardly talks to us. You try to spark up a conversation in the plaza and they don't go no further than saying, maybe, good morning. All the time we been here we haven't been invited into anybody's house, not to speak of a party or anything. When we first got here Bill he tried to strike up acquaintances here in the bar, or in the dining room. He couldn't even find anybody who'd let him buy a drink. Nobody's friendly in this town."

Her husband said, demurring slightly, "Now Martha, there was that girl in the square, the first day we arrived. She was kind of friendly. But she told us we wouldn't like it here."

"Lilith?" Alex said. "Lilith Eden?"

"That was her name I think. Since then, we've seen her around the Sierra Nevada a few times. But she just kind of nods. Never seems to have time to talk any."

"So she advised you to leave, eh? Said that you wouldn't like San Miguel. That it was too dull here."

"Yeah. And I guess she was right. We're going to leave. This town's just got no hospitality about it. I get the feeling they just don't want anybody new."

One of the other customers came to his feet and searched in his right pants pocket. He came up with a handful of coins and put four of them on the table next to the glass he had been drinking from, then added a fifth coin. Alex Germain couldn't help but notice, because the other had been drinking from the same type glass he was, that is, a brandy snifter. The four coins the other had put down were easily recognized due to their octagonal shape; they were ten peso pieces. The smaller coin was a five, undoubtedly left as a tip.

Alex glanced down, unobtrusively, at the two tabs the bartender had left on his own table. They were for eighty pesos apiece, just double the old timer's rate.

"It's kind of a strange town, all right," he said to the two Americans. "I never would have expected to find in a back woods little place like San Raphael an Austrian girl like Ursula who I'd last seen in Vienna."

"Austrian girl?" the woman said. "She's the nicest person we met in town but I wouldn't exactly call her a girl." She sniffed. "Besides, she's American. Told me herself she was from Pennsylvania."

The man was frowning too. "Austrians talk German, don't they? Miz Zavala talks American as much as you and me. Slang and everything."

"Now that you mention it," Alex said, "she does at that. Seems to have the idiom down pat." He came to his feet. "I'd better get in to my lunch. See you folks later." He fumbled in his wallet and tossed two hundred pesos to the table for drinks and tip.

The Texan stood and extended a hand for a shake. "We're the Beaumonts," he said. "Martha and Bill. Proud to meet you."

Alex shook. "Alex Germain," he said. He got the feeling that they hated to see him go, in view of the fact that he was the sole person they'd been able to talk to in a week.

He was mildly surprised to find that the copy of the *Journal of the American Gerontology Society* was gone. He had planned to appropriate it. He hadn't seen anyone pick up the publication.

The larger of the two dining rooms had thinned out in patrons, so there were only half a dozen fellow diners when he entered. The head waiter, Marcelo, Alex assumed, ushered him to a small table and let him have a menu.

He took it in. It would have been more at home in Western Europe. Only in Mexico City did you find an international selection of this variety. Well, Acapulco, perhaps.

The Hungarian goulash came with Pasta del Casa. Did Nuscha actually make her own pasta in the boondocks of the State of Guanajuato? He ordered the dish, a small mixed salad, and a beer to come immediately, when the maitre d' returned. Marcelo, it occurred to him, appeared Italian, or possibly Swiss, rather than Mexican, and was an impeccable waiter.

While he was waiting and sipping at his dark brew, he looked around at his fellows—and froze. For a long moment he stared and then hesitantly came to his feet and approached another single table, which stood before a window giving out on the patio. It was occupied by a small elderly man who had a cup of tea before him and was reading a newspaper.

Alex said, his voice unbelieving, "Herr Professor Gottlieb . . . ?"

For the first time, Alex noticed that there was a dog at the feet of the other. A short-haired, rusty-gold hound, his hindquarters under the table. He looked up and growled very softly in query.

The small man said, "That will be all, Buda." He looked up at Alex. "I am afraid you have the advantage of me, sir." His tone was impatient.

Alex said, "Aren't you Dr. Werner Gottlieb, of the University of Vienna? I once covered a symposium which you chaired, oh, many years ago. I thought I had read that you had since . . . uh, passed away."

"I am afraid the report was grossly exaggerated then, young man. I am retired. If you are a journalist, I most certainly have nothing for you. I can't think of anything newsworthy in which I have participated for many years. And now if . . ."

Alex said, "But this is like old home week. Nuscha, that is Ursula Richter . . . Well, Señora

Zavala these days. She's the owner of the Sierra Nevada. She used to be manager of the Theresien Pension, across from the school. You used to come in every day and play chess and drink coffee with the other professors. I interviewed you. You were the chairman of the symposium on gerontology that I was in town to write about."

The older man looked impatient. "I am afraid that there is no great mystery. Frau Zavala is an old friend, as you say from the days when I taught. We corresponded, even after she removed here to Mexico. Upon my retirement, she urged that I come to San Raphael. The suggestion was quite apt. I find all my requirements met." His eyes were chilly. "Including being free of journalists and others who would intrude upon my desired solitude. You might say that I am a bit of a recluse, sir. And now, if you will pardon me."

The dog came to its feet and headed for the door.

Alex said, "Sorry to bother you, Professor. We had become quite friendly in Vienna."

"I am afraid I don't recall you whatsoever." The professor arose to his feet and followed after the dog. Seemingly, his bill was already paid, or possibly he had a charge account.

The dog came to the door, looked up and down quickly and then dropped back to walk alongside his master. It was a Vizsla, Alex recognized, vaguely. A Hungarian hunting dog which would go possibly seventy-five pounds. He couldn't remember ever having seen one in the United States, not to speak of Mexico. They were a breed seldom found outside the Balkans.

"Well, that was a slap in the face," he muttered.

He could see through the window the Austrian crossing the patio, his cane swinging jauntily, as though it was an affectation, rather than a need. It brought home to Alex Germain something that he, in his surprise at seeing the other, had forgotten. When he had spoken to Herr Professor Werner Gottlieb last, the man had appeared to be possibly in his mid-seventies. He didn't look older now.

Interlude

When the phone screen lit up, disclosing the familiar face, she said, "Bertrand. Greetings. How does the ball bounce?"

He smiled at her, affection there, and said, "Peachy dandy. How are things down there?"

"Routine. Well, until what I'm calling you about developed. It's probably not important."

"At your service."

"I'd like you to check this out in the International Data Banks. Not too long before he retired, Werner chaired a symposium on gerontology at the university. At the time, it received quite a bit of publicity. The subject did, in those days. The reporter who covered it for the *London Illustrated News* was named Alexander Germain. He might have written under Alex . . ."

"How do you spell Germain?" The efficient looking, early middle aged man she had called was obviously making notes.

"I don't know."

"No strain. There's not many alternative ways it might be spelled. Go on."

"I want you to find out what you can about him.

Everything. I assume the place to start would be the magazine."

"Ummm. Getting a complete report on him will probably take a bit of time, Liebchen, but I can probably give you what the *London Illustrated News* has in moments."

"I'll hang on."

She sat there and waited. Drummed her fingers on the desk before her for a time. Inspected her nails for a time. And sighed a few times.

Bertrand's face reappeared on the screen. He was frowning. He said, "The *News* didn't cover the event, I'm afraid. I'm not surprised; it's not exactly their cup of tea."

She stared at him. "It couldn't have been the cheapest thing in the world to have him sent to Vienna and kept him there for a week and then not to use his stories and interviews."

He said, "Possibly he was getting the coverage for some other publication. I'm checking it out."

She said doubtfully, "He said the *London Illustrated News*. I know the magazine. It was quite popular in those days."

He looked down, obviously checking something. "The meeting was fairly well publicized by the British press but his by-line doesn't appear on any of the articles."

She looked surprised. "Possibly he used a pseudonym. Well, let's take it from this angle. In those days, all hotel and pension registrations had to be listed with the Austrian Interior Police. Check their archives and see if he's registered during that period at the Theresien Pension."

She waited again. This time a bit less patiently. Her expression was puzzled.

Bertrand came back on finally and said, "He was registered, all right. Alexander Germain."

She thought of something and said, "Under what kind of passport?"

"Costa Rican."

"Costa Rican! Isn't that one of the countries where, if you're educated enough to sign your name on the application and have three photographs and the fee, they'll give a passport to anybody?"

"Yes," he said. "Do you want the passport number? It was issued in 1975."

She thought about it. "No. It's too long ago to attempt to check from that end. Those Central American countries aren't noted for their accuracy. Look, can you check out journalists in general? Are there any statistics on articles published and who wrote them?"

"Of course. What countries?"

"Why, I'd think the United Kingdom and the United States first."

"Hold on. Alexander Germain, or Alex Germain. You're sure he's English speaking, of course?"

"He says he's an American and these days talks like one, just as we do, but he has an international air about him. One that I can't put my finger on. He's certainly not Germanic."

"You surprise me, Liebling. I thought you were infallible in such things."

"Stop calling me darling, or I won't sleep with you the next time I see you."

He grinned. "My wife wouldn't allow it anyway. Hold on. This won't take long."

It didn't. He came back in a few minutes. His face was more quizzical than before.

He shook his head negatively and said, "There simply isn't any writer named Alexander Germain, either non-fiction or fiction, who has ever written for an English language publication. And his name isn't listed as one who writes under any pseudonym. The nearest name to it is an Alan German and he's only been writing for the past eight years."

She looked at him dumbly.

He grimaced and said, "Want me to keep working on trying to locate this guy? Among other things, I can check back on Costa Rica, though I doubt if it would do any good."

She nodded. "It might be more important than I first thought, Bertrand."

Chapter 2

The longing for immortality is as nearly universal as anything we know pertaining to the inner wishes of human beings; but some men, from time to time, have renounced any interest in the subject of immortality. They are lost, however, in the vastness of the general Quest.
—Norman Cousins
The Celebration of Life

1.

The lunch had been superb. Perhaps Nuscha's presence in the Sierra Nevada kitchen made all the difference since usually Mexican cooks were inadequate with international dishes. He couldn't recall having eaten a better goulash since last he was in Hungary, nor better pasta since he had lived in Italy. And the small mixed salad was perfection

34

with its ultra-fresh salad vegetables. He finished with a Napoleon dessert, though he didn't truly have capacity for it. He hadn't touched such a whipped cream pastry since Demel's on Kohlmarkt near the Hofburg. That centuries old Viennese Konditorei perhaps served the best pastry, ice-cream and schlagobers in Europe but Nuscha rivaled its Napoleon.

Between his two pre-luncheon cognacs, his two strong beers with his meal and the heavy and rich food itself, Alex Germain was on the glassy-eyed side by the time he called it quits and headed for his room. He was not ordinarily a devotee to the Spanish-Mexican institution of the siesta but this was an exception and particularly in view of his hours upon a second class bus, some of them standing.

He nodded to Marcelo, who stood in the doorway, on his way out and said, "Excellent."

The maitre d' smiled. Oh, he was a pro, all right, all right. He enjoyed seeing a well fed guest. "Thank you, señor," he murmured in reply. "The Señora mentioned that you were acquainted with cuisine."

He retraced the route Nuscha had taken him along earlier. The steps led to no other destination than his oversized room.

He kicked off his shoes and sprawled out on the bed. It was summer and there was no need of even a spread over him. He dropped off in minutes, wondering as he did whether or not Professor Gottlieb could have possibly been as old as Alex had thought when last they had met in Vienna.

He slept longer than he had expected, though,

come to think of it, he'd had no particular intentions when he had dozed off.

He swung his legs out over the side of the bed and shook his head. He was still feeling somewhat food-logged. It was fairly dark in the room, the sole light coming from the patio below his windows.

So evening was upon him. He had expected to go out on the town. However, tomorrow was another day. Tonight, he'd check out the Sierra Nevada a bit more. It was a rather strange layout to be in a one horse Mexican town such as this. You might have expected the equivalent in France, Portugal or Italy, but hardly here.

As he passed the dining rooms, on his way to the patio, he noted that, as before, the guests seemed to be elderly types. He suspected that they blessed the presence of Nuscha Zavala in their little retirement center. Without her oasis, the amenities would be rather slim in San Raphael.

The patio was elegantly and quietly lit with unobtrusive bulbs, here and there. The flowers and ferns were as attractive at night as they had been during the day.

Marcelo and one of his waiters were busy putting up tables outside the bar entrance. There were already a half dozen occupied. It gave an air somewhat similar to a sidewalk cafe in one of the European capitals. The balmy evening was certainly such that it was called for. From the door of the cocktail lounge issued forth piano music. Inwardly, he smiled. It was an old tune. "There's a Long, Long Trail a Winding." He hadn't heard it for years.

The Beaumonts, Bill and Martha, who had been

looking for a house to buy, were at one of the outside tables, cocktails before them. They'd been looking rather glum until they spotted him. Now, Bill waved frantically and made a gesture inviting him over. However, Alex pretended not to notice the invitation and simply smiled and waved back. He had no intentions of killing the evening listening to their complaints of San Raphael.

Inside, he could see the reason why Marcelo was putting up tables in the patio. The place was packed. He stood there a moment and looked about. And was again taken aback by the sameness of the occupants. As in the dining room, practically everybody seemed between the ages of sixty and seventy. Oh, there were a few exceptions. The energetic pianist, now launched into "Only Make Believe", that Show Boat hit of the thirties, was about Alex's own age. And there were three or four others, spotted about the room, all women he noted, who were possibly no older than their fifties.

Practically every chair was taken and he turned to go back to the patio, in hopes of finding room there. However, from the far side of the lounge someone waved to him. He frowned and peered, the dim light making it difficult to make her out. Was it Nuscha? He would have expected her to be occupied in the kitchen or dining room.

But no. It came to him. The young woman in the park. Lilith—what was it?—Lilith Eden, slowly dying of boredom in the sleepy Mexican pueblo.

He crossed over to her, swiveling through the tightly packed chairs and tables. She was seated alone on one of the small sofas.

He grinned at her and said, "I'll buy you a drink in return for a seat."

"The seat's on the house," she told him, patting the space next to her. "Besides, I should be the one who buys the drink. It's a life saver in this ghost town to talk to somebody new."

He took the place and looked about again. He said, under his breath, "Is there some law that states that everybody has to be the same age?"

"You'd damn well think so," she said bitterly. She took a sip from her wine glass. It occured to him that she didn't seem the type that drank white wine in a bar. In fact, given her sour disposition, he wondered that it wasn't boiler makers she was knocking back.

He looked about again. Everybody else seemed to be drinking either wine, beer or limeade. He'd at first thought of either gin or vodka and tonic, but the glasses were too large. Lime or lemonade it must be.

Then another thing came to him. Nobody was smoking. In fact, now that he checked, there were no ash trays on any of the tables. In a bar? Now he had seen everything. It was all right with him, since he didn't smoke himself.

Paco came up and Alex said, "Cognac, please."

"It was Martell, wasn't it, señor?"

"That's right."

Alex noted for the first time that Werner Gottlieb was sitting, alone, at the tiny table next to them. He bowed his head in greeting and the Austrian gave a slight nod in return. There was a cup of tea before him.

Alex looked down. Gottlieb's dog was stretched

out on the floor, as in the dining room earlier, half under the table, for protection against being stepped upon, undoubtedly.

Alex said, "Hello, Buddha."

The animal, who'd been resting with his hound's chin on his front paws, looked up and contemplated him for a moment and then gave his tail a begrudging half wag.

The pianist finished "Bye Bye Blackbird" and launched into "Me and My Shadow".

Alex took up the drink the waiter served and savored the aroma. "He doesn't look old enough to remember that one," he said to the girl.

"Happily, Jack can play anything," she told him. "Even for this crowd. He's the latest addition to the community. Why he stays, I'll never know. If he doesn't look out, he'll wind up like all the rest, sitting around listening to his arteries harden. But wait until he does 'After the Ball Is Over'. We'll probably have a sing-along."

She almost hit it on the nailhead. But the song that loosened them up was "I Wonder Who's Kissing Her Now", from approximately the same period. Several at a table down from Alex and Lilith joined in with the words. Then, about the room, several more contributed.

> "I wonder who's buying the wine,
> For lips that I used to call mine.
> I wonder if she
> Ever tells him of me.
> I wonder who's kissing her now."

Alex was amused but then something came to him. It must be his imagination but he got the feeling that the voices he was hearing seemed younger than the persons singing. A bit too robust, a bit too sprightly for people in their sixties or more. He shrugged it off and looked about the room again.

He said to Lilith, "This is obviously a gringo hangout. I can make out only two who might be Mexicans."

She nodded. "Most of the locals can't afford Ursula's damned prices. But that one, sitting with the Chinese, is David Cohen. He's the presidenté, mayor, we'd call it, and also owns half the town property."

"Cohen? He looks Mexican."

"He is," she said. "The story is that his ancestor came over at the time of the Conquest, fleeing the Inquisition in Spain. Once in Mexico, he found the holy fathers, complete with their thumb screws and such, were only a few months behind him. So he left Mexico City and continued fleeing up here to the then wild north. Since there weren't exactly a surplus of nice Jewish girls around, he did the next best thing and married a nice Aztec girl. After several generations of that he obviously is as mestizo as anybody else."

He was intrigued. "But he's still Jewish as far as religion is concerned?"

The sides of her mouth turned down in her half smile of deprecation. "How the hell would I know? When it comes to religion, I'm not even an atheist. But instead of a coat of arms over his doorway, he has a Star of David. Considering the history of his family, I rather doubt that he's a devout Catholic."

"And that Chinese, or Japanese, he's talking to. Is he Mexican too?"

"Damned if I know. Hsu Fu, being Oriental, is inscrutable. Along with Señor Cohen, he's one of the town's top property owners. Why the two of them would want to possess all these ruins, is a mystery."

Alex looked at her from the side of his eyes. "You mean they own most of the banged-up houses in San Raphael? You'd have to go to one or the other of them if you wanted to buy a ruin and fix it up?"

She grimaced, but on her it looked good. "Take a friend's word for it. Don't even think about it. You'd die from ennui before the year was out."

He said, musingly, "Then, if those two didn't want you to settle in San Raphael, you simply couldn't get a place, eh?"

She didn't bother to answer.

Alex felt something cold touch his hand and started. He looked down. It was the nose of Gottlieb's dog. The hound was looking up at him, his eyes as dark golden as his hair.

Gottlieb said, "Buda, that will be all."

Alex said, "He's all right. Nice dog."

The elderly scientist said, an edge of impatience there, "He wants you to scratch his back."

Alex complied and was rewarded with a double wag of the stubby tail.

Alex said, "Not exactly a one man dog, is he?"

Gottlieb grunted and said, "He's a Hungarian," as though that explained everything.

Alex continued the scratching and said, "Buddha? He doesn't exactly look the type to be named after Gautama."

"Buda," the Austrian explained, grudgingly,

perhaps. "He had a sister named Pest. In short, Budapest. He's a Vizsla, one of the world's oldest breeds. They came from Siberia with the Magyars. War dogs, to begin with, but then when the Magyars settled down in Hungary, they became hunting dogs, retrievers. They were used during the Middle Ages, in particular in falconry."

As a matter of fact, Alex Germain was acquainted with those details but he welcomed the opportunity of opening the old man up to conversation.

He said, "You don't see the breed in the States."

Gottlieb nodded agreement to that. "You seldom saw them out of Hungary before the Second World War. The aristocrats kept them rather secluded. Something like the Weimaraners in Germany. But when the communists moved in, some of the nobility that escaped took their best dogs with them. A few finally wound up in the United States and the breed was admitted to the American Kennel Club in 1960. However, as you say, you still don't see many in America."

The scientist clicked his teeth together as though suddenly realizing he was talking to someone he hadn't planned to. He looked at his wristwatch and said, "I suppose I should be having my dinner."

He came to his feet and said, "Come along Buda."

The dog sighed but obeyed. In fact, he beat his master to the door and looked out of it, up and down the patio, before emerging. Professor Gottlieb followed after.

Alex motioned with a finger for Paco to bring them another brandy and white wine. As it arrived, a newcomer entered and made her way to the piano. The pianist looked up at her and gave her a sly grin and launched into the lilting "The Girl I Left Behind Me". The lush young woman smiled back and sank into a chair near the piano bench.

One of the men who had earlier participated in singing "I Wonder Who's Kissing Her Now" joined in with a really excellent tenor.

> *". . . I knew her heart was breaking,*
> *And to my heart in anguish pressed,*
> *The girl I left behind me."*

"Jesus," Alex muttered. "They even remember Civil War tunes. Wasn't that the marching song Custer's Seventh Cavalry rode out to on their way to their rendezvous with the Sioux at the Little Bighorn?"

Lilith was taking him in. "You seem to be rather knowledgeable about the old songs yourself."

"Kind of a hobby," he told her. "I'm a buff."

The girl—woman, actually—was the Black Irish type, he decided. Or possibly Welsh. Yes, Welsh. Very black hair, delicate complexion, generous mouth, faultless white teeth, perfectly shaped ears. A figure voluptuous and possibly just past its peak—but, on the other hand, possibly not. She was dressed in rather tight black slacks and wore a light black turtleneck sweater.

"I see you have a rival, Nefertiti," he said.

"How was that?"

"You're not the only beautiful woman in town."

She said, "Oh. That's Fay Morgan. Anybody who'd settle down to a librarian's job in a ruin of a village like this . . ." She cut herself short, as though she'd been saying something she shouldn't.

"Librarian?" he said. "You mean you have a library in San Raphael?"

She shrugged shapely shoulders. "Such as it is. Supported by the foreign community. When one kicks off, his books are usually donated to the library. When it comes to novels you have a selection that includes *Moby Dick, Ben Hur,* and Alcott's *Little Women.* Nothing more recent."

Time seemed to pass gently away, Mexican style. He had no appetite. His late, heavy mid-day meal was still lasting. Usually, he wasn't a big eater. Alex Germain had another Martell and then another.

Somewhere along the line, Lilith said scornfully, "Well, this is it. This is the town action. I warned you."

"It's not so bad," he protested.

She twisted her mouth at that opinion. "Stick around here for a year or so and you'll wither away like the rest of these fogies."

"I still don't see why you stay, if hate it this much."

"I'm wanted by the FBI. And they'd never think to look for me here. According to their records, I'm not that far around the bend."

Slowly the room emptied as the occupants either drifted into the dining room for dinner, or called it a night and evidently went on to their respective homes. Lilith stuck it out as long as he did.

However, he yawned finally and said, "It's this altitude. I'm sleepy. I think I'll go on back to bed, Lilith."

"You'll want to get rested up for that bus trip

tomorrow," she agreed. "Well, thanks for the most exciting date I've had for years."

He looked at her and laughed, even as he stood. "If you don't get out of San Raphael yourself, soon, you're going to go up the wall. Why don't you go on back to the States and shoot it out with the FBI?"

"I just might do that," she told him.

Returning to his room, he could feel the alcohol he had taken on. As the seasoned traveler he was, he should have remembered that the first few days, when you are over a mile high, cut your tolerance for liquor by half. After you'd become acclimated, you returned to your normal regime, but for about a week, if you were normally a six drink an evening man, you'd best cut it back to three. Otherwise, you'd find yourself nicely smashed on what ordinarily you'd never think of as excessive boozing.

In his room, he didn't bother to switch on the lights. There was still a bit of illumination from the patio. He drew the drapes on the windows that overlooked it and, yawning, began to strip. He had pajamas in his bag but didn't bother to root them out. In this climate, it'd be a pleasure to sleep in the buff.

He had expected to fall off into slumber immediately but it didn't come. His mind went back over the time since he'd arrived on the bus. That San Raphael was an off-beat town wasn't a conclusion difficult to come to. Certainly it was no paragon of hospitality. If his old acquaintance, Nuscha Richter, hadn't been run into, he probably would have gained the same impressions that the Texas couple had, particularly after being subjected to Lilith

Eden's bad mouthing of the community and its inhabitants.

Yes, the day had been interesting, particularly the last few hours in the bar. It wasn't just that none of the foreign colony wore glasses, save for Bill Beaumont and he couldn't really be considered in their number. But none of the men were even partially bald, though some were gray. Nor had he seen any signs of hearing aids, though, of course, these days the instruments were usually quite inconspicuous. And, come to think of it, none, men nor women, seemed to have dentures. Not from what he could observe. But then, the room had been fairly dark and he couldn't see much in the way of facial details at the farther tables. But he would have sworn that none of the bar's habitués boasted false teeth. If they did, it was really superlative work.

Yes, a fascinating colony of retirees.

He caught a movement from the side of his eyes.

The French windows of his room which faced on the extensive terrace were undraped. He had pulled the curtains on the windows overlooking the patio but there had been no need to in the other direction. The balcony was rather dark but still he had seen something move out there. By this time, his eyes had become adjusted to the gloom of his room. He squinted. It was a figure, moving slowly, gliding might be the term, near one of the terrace tables.

It seemed to be garbed, from head to ankles, in a black cloak. A hooded cloak. A woman's hooded opera cloak? It was too dark to make out any detail whatsoever.

The figure was moving toward the French windows.

He had no sort of weapon, either in his clothes, which he had flung over the chair next to his bed, nor in his luggage. Long since, electronic surveillance of international travelers had been extended from airline passengers to those who travelled by train, bus or private vehicle. And he had no intention of being picked up for interrogation by border guards discovering a gun, or even an outsized pocket knife.

He considered, momentarily, jumping from the bed and taking up a small table or, better still, a straight chair, in lieu of a weapon. But no. He raised himself on one elbow, covered only by a bedsheet. The Mexican morning would undoubtedly be chilly eight hours from now but at this time of night the heat of the day still held on.

The windows leading onto the terrace didn't even squeak as they were pushed open and the vague figure noiselessly slipped through. Had he been asleep, he could never have known of the intrusion. He simply reclined there and watched. He could see, now, even less detail than when his visitor had still been out in the faint light of the stars and the sliver of moon at this time of the month.

It paused momentarily and at first he didn't realize that the cloak was being removed. But then the figure was suddenly draped in white, rather than in black. And . . . and unless he was mistaken, it was the form of a woman.

He sucked in air. The garb, of course, was a nightgown.

For only the briefest of moments did he consider

whether or not one of his fellow hotel guests was sleepwalking. Don't be naive, Alex Germain.

He moved not at all, as she gently pulled back the sheet and gracefully slipped in beside him.

He began to say, "Who . . ."

But she put a finger over his lips. In the all but complete dark he couldn't make out her face whatsoever.

In his time, Alex Germain had been around. He had enjoyed his share of women. As a matter of fact, he wasn't aware of the reality, but the average woman, on romance bent, was inclined to prefer him to the ultra-endowed masculine types personified by the sex symbols of New Hollywood and Tri-Di City, recently developed on Long Island. He had a pleasantness, rather than an aggressiveness, in the play play between the sexes and it seemed to pay off. Yes, in his time Alex had not suffered from lack of feminine companionship and horizontal refreshments. However, offhand he could not recall ever having been so titillated as by the strangeness of this encounter.

There could be no question whatsoever as to her intentions. She touched him, held him, expertly. There was no question about his coming to raging erection. There need be no build-up to it. He was all but instantly ready for completion. Preliminary love-play was as unnecessary for him as it seemingly was for her.

She was mature. Certainly she was no child, no girl, nor even a young woman. Her body was in the full glory of its mature femininity. Her breasts, her belly, her buttocks. He entered her as deeply as he could ever remember having penetrated

sexually. Which seemingly didn't make sense ...
but did. The act was complete. So very complete.
The very complete coming together of man and
woman. He ejaculated bountifully almost immediately but still not so soon as to thwart her needs.
Her scream at climax was soft but from the soul.

He dropped back onto his pillow. In spite of the
short duration of the act, he felt drained. He had
never quite experienced anything comparable.

She was stroking the sparse hair on his chest.

Again, he tried to see her face and couldn't make
it out in the shadows. He couldn't even tell if she
was blond or brunette. He refrained from snap-
ping on the bedlight. Obviously, that was the last
thing she wished. He didn't get it, but then, who
was he to protest?

He said, "What's your name?"

Her tinkle of laugh was so low as hardly to be
heard. And her voice low and sultry and as though
it was being disguised. "Dulcinea will do."

Her hand had wandered down from his chest,
expertly again.

He pulled in air. This time, undoubtedly, things
would not proceed quite so fast.

2.

Alex Germain couldn't later remember when he
had at long last fallen off. It couldn't have been too
very much before dawn. When he finally awakened,
the day was advanced. Light streaked in through
the French windows, which were open. There was
no sign of she who had named herself Dulcinea.

No sign of her cloak, nor anything else to indicate that she had been there at all.

Almost, he wondered if he could have been dreaming, assisted perhaps by the drinks of the day and night before. But no, he couldn't have dreamed himself into this state of lethargy. He tried to remember, but couldn't, the number of times she had brought him to orgasm. Whatever the number, it was beyond that of which he would have ever thought himself capable. He wasn't the satyr type. He had never thought of himself as a lascivious man. Sex was sex and he was all in favor of it but not to the point of feeling like a boneless eunuch at dawning.

He forced himself from the bed and staggered, rather than walked, to the bathroom. The showers, both hot and cold, revived him but partially. He returned to his bag and located razor and toothbrush.

Later he dressed in the same clothing he had worn the evening preceding, save for clean socks though his laundry wasn't a problem thus far. He had come down from the States fairly directly and, wearing sturdy traveling clothes, hadn't soiled much thus far save socks and handkerchiefs.

He went out onto the terrace and looked about it more carefully than he had the day before with Nuscha. To the left of the French windows was a small iron staircase which spiraled upward to the roof. He walked around the parapet of the large balcony, looking over. One side had the Sierra Nevada's patio down below. The rear, affording its view of the town's center including the rearing church towers, had, immediately below, the once garden of what had long ago been a majestic home. The place was now in such ruin that not even poverty stricken squatters inhabited its roofless rooms. It would have taken a rather sizeable ladder to have ascended to his terrace from the barren garden, a ladder clumsier and weighter than he could picture she who had called herself Dulcinea managing very easily, particularly in view of the fact that she had been barefooted.

The other side of the terrace overlooked another patio, one considerably smaller than that boasted by the Sierra Nevada and obviously belonging to the next door residence. The same sort of ladder would have been necessary to have come up from it.

He rubbed the back of his hand over his mouth thoughtfully and ascended the narrow iron staircase leading to the roof.

The hotel's roof was sizeable and obviously periodically used for sun bathing and possibly even parties. There were a few pieces of porch furniture about and three or four air mattresses. Toward the other end of it was the entry to what was obviously a stairway leading below. The only other access to the roof, so far as he could see, save for the circular iron one leading down to his balcony. He estimated that the stairway would be above the dining room, two levels below. He had seen no indication of such a stairway in the hotel dining room and assumed that it went down only as far as the second floor.

He walked over to the side of the roof and looked out upon the adjoining top of the building next door. It was obviously not so extensive a place as that from which the Sierra Nevada had been reconstructed. The roof boasted a multitude of potted plants, two clothes lines and a pila where the maid undoubtedly did by hand the household laundry. Not for San Raphael such foofaraw as a washing machine. The top of the house opposite was approximately two feet below that of the Sierra Nevada and there was absolutely nothing to prevent anyone from crossing from one building to the other. Unless it was Buda, who Alex could make out lying between two of the potted geraniums enjoying the morning sun.

Alex looked at him for a moment and then called softly, "Hi, Buda."

The dog had been watching him. Now it sighed, let its red tongue hang out, and offered a slight wag of its clipped tail but didn't come to its feet. Alex wondered how the hound would react if he crossed over to the other's territory. He also wondered how long the animal had been there. Was this Gottlieb's home and did Buda spend his nights on the roof guarding access to the house? And, if so, had the dog seen Dulcinea come and go on her way to his bed? It was seemingly quite possible that this was her route.

Quite possible, but there was no evidence it was true. He turned and headed for the stairway.

As he had assumed, it led down to a hallway that extended the better part of the length of the building. Doors opened off to both left and right, five of them. No, six. The five, he assumed led to other rooms and suites. His own quarters, with his private entrance, were completely separated from them though all were on the same floor. The sixth and smaller door was probably a broom closet, storage space for the room maid. Just in the way of experiment, he tried the door. It was locked.

He looked at the other doors thoughtfully and wondered if they were as well. He didn't try them in view of the fact that he had no idea if there were any other guests besides himself. Well, himself and the Beaumonts. From what he had gathered, they were staying here too, though nobody had said so. The Sierra Nevada was the only hostelry in town suitable for gringos. At any rate, he had no excuse for barging into occupied quarters, if they were unlocked or no.

Why lock a broom closet, if that was what it was? If the crime rate in this sleepy Mexican pueblo was so small that hotel rooms went unlocked, why bar a broom closet?

He walked the length of the hall and looked out the window there. There were iron bars beyond the glass, which was routine for San Raphael. The window looked down upon Calle Hospicio. At this time of the morning, there was nothing to be seen in the street.

Alex reversed himself and headed down for the opposite end of the corridor where there was another staircase, somewhat more ornate than the one which led to the roof, wider and with gray carpeting similar to that in the hall and that covering both the dining room and bar floors.

The stairway led out onto the patio at the opposite end from the street entrance, the dining rooms and the bar. However, it was not quite all the way down the gardens. He continued his exploration and found another door, very well done in antique carved wood. He looked up. His own room and terrace were immediately above.

He pushed open the door and entered. The chamber beyond was large, larger than the two dining rooms put together. It was out of proportion in as small an establishment as the Sierra Nevada and looked as though it was seldom if ever put to use. There was a dais at one end of the hall with a speaker's podium on it. Scattered around, haphazardly, were a few tables and chairs. Other folding chairs were stacked against the walls. It was a bit more stark than the public rooms of the pasada. However, this was relieved somewhat by three large picture windows which faced out on the gardens.

A voice from behind him said, "What were you looking for, Alex?"

He turned. It was Ursula Zavala, done today in a striking Austrian dirndl. The tyrolian dress with its full skirt and close-fitting bodice, with its colorful and striking patterned material, well set off her excellent tall figure. She was frowning and fingering her sole gold earring. He remembered the gesture now from of old, a nervous mannerism.

He said, "Hi, Nuscha. Just casing the joint. You've got a beautiful place here."

"If you mean the Sierra Nevada as a whole, thanks. If you mean this monstrosity of a hall, you're exaggerating."

He looked about again. Set up correctly, the place would have easily sat two hundred persons. "What's it for?" he said.

"I call it Eduardo's folly. When he renovated the building, he joined several of the old rooms together. It was to be for conventions, banquets, weddings, even dances. Where he thought they were going to come from, I don't know."

He looked about some more. "Why don't you convert the space to extra suites, or rooms, or a larger dining room?"

She snorted at him and turned to leave as though expecting him to follow. "In the first place, I can't keep filled the suites I've got. The same applies to the dining rooms. In the second place, I couldn't afford it. I operate on a shoestring."

Out in the patio she turned and looked him over, scowling. "You look awful," she said. "Hangover?"

"Not exactly. I didn't get too much sleep last night."

"You look as though you've been pulled through the proverbial wringer." Her voice went mocking and her laugh wrinkles were there at the side of her eyes. "I noticed you with Lilith last night. You're not that fast an operator, are you?"

"With Lilith? She's so acid, she'd burn the end of it off if you stuck it in her."

She had to laugh but she said, "Hey, watch your language. We didn't know each other that well in Vienna."

He did a burlesque leer. "It was pretty well."

She had closed the door behind them. Now she said, "Alex, why are you here?"

He looked at her. "How do you mean?"

"You said you were a writer. Last time I saw you, you were in Vienna. A writer, who does the international scene, doesn't travel around like a tourist between assignments. I'd think second class traveling would be the last thing he'd do in the way of fun. But, even if so, why in the world come to San Raphael? There hasn't been a story here since Pancho Villa shot up the town almost a century ago."

"Oh, I don't know. I find the place kind of interesting. I might get a saleable piece out of it. Bunch of retired duffers settled down in this all but forgotten Spanish Colonial town. Very picturesque, perfect climate, nice scenery. I figured on spending today just wandering around and getting the feel of the area."

They were walking slowly, side by side, in the direction of the dining room.

"There is no feel to San Raphael, except kind of a dusty one," she told him. "However, I'll have Paco, or one of the other boys, guide you around. See the market, the Zócalo, a couple of the churches. That's about all there is."

"I'd rather do it on my own," he said. "Just drifting about waiting for something to happen to surprise me."

"Nobody's been surprised in San Raphael since ..."

"I know, I know, since Montezuma stubbed his toe down in the square. Lady, what this town needs is a public relations bureau. After listening to you, the Beaumonts and Lilith Eden, I'd think even the rats would leave. Kind of like deserting a sinking ship."

They'd arrived at the dining room door.

She came out with it, of a sudden. "Look, Alex," she said, a trace of urgency there. "I haven't had a vacation for over a year. I've got a car. What say we take off? Today. Practically right now. We'll drive down to Manzanilla. The beaches there are fine. We'll spend a few days, perhaps a week, sitting in the sun. Eating the shrimp and crab and crawfish tails, drinking the cold beer. We'll have a ball of a time. Then we'll each go on our own way. You to wherever the road takes you. Me back here. Oh God, it sounds wonderful. You can't imagine how I need a vacation from this graveyard."

He looked at her. "Isn't this rather sudden, my fair beauty?"

There was a glint in her Teutonic blue eyes. A cold glint. "It was you who was telling me about our prolonged evening in Vienna, starting off in the Rathaus Keller. This would be sort of a second chapter to that short-lived romance."

He said slowly, "Why don't you want me to see San Raphael, Nuscha?"

"Why . . . why, don't be ridiculous, you . . . you clod."

He looked after her as she flounced off in the direction of the swinging doors of the kitchen. The peasant dress accentuated her mature femininity. Her buttocks were superb. Alex Germain sighed. Hadn't he been utterly drained, he might have considered her propositon. The way he felt now, he would have equally turned down Cleopatra, Helen of Troy, or even the more recent Sophia Loren.

He turned and entered the dining room, wondering if they were still serving breakfast. Seemingly they were. The Beaumonts were seated at a table for two, about half way through their morning repast.

He said, "Top of the day," and took the table

next to them. There was a small, typed menu on the plate and he took it up.

Martha Beaumont looked at Alex critically. She said, "You look sort of peaked."

Alex said, "The altitude affects people differently. I suppose I should have taken it easier last night with the booze."

A Mexican girl, complete with colored ribbons in her braids, came to take his order. Evidently, she doubled as a waitress for the breakfast trade before Marcelo and other waiters came on.

He had deliberately missed supper the night before and was now famished. Of course, the siege with Dulcinea hadn't exactly dulled his appetite either. He ordered a fruit plate, a double order of eggs Rancheros style, fried beans, toast, mango marmalada and coffee con leche.

When the girl was gone, Bill Beaumont said, "That shindig last night was the biggest turnout we seen in this town. That is, since the first night we checked in. Seems as if the whole of the San Raphael foreign colony was here. Now you come and they all turn out again."

Alex said, "I've gotten the impression that most entertainment takes place in the private homes. Card games, dinners, cocktail parties and so forth. From what you say, it sounds as though when somebody new does check in, a rare occasion, they all turn out here at the Sierra Nevada to give them the once over."

The Texan hesitated before taking a bite of the toast he had half way to his mouth. "That's the way it looks all right. But I guess it's just coincidence, like. They sure as the dickens don't act like they want any newcomers in the community."

Alex had the feeling that the two lonely Texans stretched out their meal, probably for the sake of someone with whom to talk. However, eventually they left after telling him effusively that they'd have to get together later, "And bend a few elbows," as Bill put it.

He managed to eat all the breakfast he had ordered and dawdled only shortly over a last coffee, taken black this time, and then decided to get about the business of checking out the pueblo of San Raphael.

On leaving the hotel, he turned right on Calle Hospicio rather than retracing the route he had taken the day before. He walked down to the end of the long block to Calle de Allende and turned right again. If his knob-o'-location served him, it should take him into the Zócalo and the town center.

It did and he hesitated for a moment under a bronze statue of Fray Raphael, after whom the town had been named. The square across the street was not so crowded as the day before. Seemingly, whatever fiesta had then been going on was now over. The food stands, for instance, were gone.

He shrugged. One route was as good as another. He had no town plan and doubted if there was one. He continued on, walking beneath the portico that shaded the sidewalk before the Spanish Colonial buildings on this side of the plaza. The shops and stalls were typically Mexican. A noisy bar, a small news and magazine shop, a barber shop, a tienda offering everything from tortillas to an endless variety of chilis, a tiny restaurant with simmering stews and soups in the window, another bar, another tienda, this time specializing in fruits and vegetables. The sidewalk was crowded with Mexicans in their daily garb, rather than the finery of the day before. He noted, all over again, that their average height could not be more than a bit over five feet. The low protein diet, undoubtedly. The average Mexican proletarian could afford little meat.

Towering a foot or more above the other pedestrians, he spotted who was obviously an equally tall fellow foreigner coming toward him. He recognized the face but for the moment couldn't place it. Thus far, he had met practically no one in San Raphael. But then it came to him. The pianist last night.

The other approached and grinned at him, extending a hand.

"Buenos días, and welcome to San Raphael. You can have it," he said. "I noticed you last night with Lilith at the hoe-down. We don't get many strangers in town." He shook Alex's hand with quick jerks and added, "I'm Jack Fast." He had a somewhat fox-like face, a slyness there.

Alex said, "Alex Germain. I enjoyed your repertoire. I haven't heard some of those tunes for so long I'd forgotten I knew them."

They backed up against the building to get out of the flow of human traffic.

The pianist grinned again. "Don't think I haven't got my work cut out remembering some of them. But that's what the old farts want and a bar music-box player has to produce what the cash customers want or out he goes."

Alex said, "I understand that was a good turnout last night."

The other let air from his long nose in contempt. "Yeah, the biggest night for months. I don't know why I stay in this endsville. Christ, if it wasn't for Ursula and Lilith and one or two others, I'd get the blue spiders. I'm warning you, Alex, get out of town quick or you'll start growing moss."

Alex laughed. "That's what everybody keeps telling me. Why do you stay on if it's so dead? You look as though you'd want more action."

Jack Fast laughed too. He was obviously the laughing type, hail fellow well met. Alex supposed it went with the trade. Who'd put up with a dead eye in a piano bar?

Fast said, "Don't kid yourself. Señora Zavala gave me a break and a job when I was flatto but as soon as I get enough of a stake I'm shaking this town's dust so fast it'll look like a storm in the Sahara. Where you from, Alex?"

It was the invariable question when American met American abroad and under the circumstances wasn't considered to come under the head of prying. "California."

"Oh, whereabouts?"

"Little town up in the San Joaquin valley. You've never heard of it."

"I know California pretty well."

"Not this town. Where're you from?"

"Brooklyn. I was on my way to Acapulco when I stopped off here. Worst mistake I ever made. What're you doing, just passing through? Tourist?"

"Yeah. When the bus stopped here, it looked interesting, so I decided to drop off and look it over."

"Well, there's nothing to see. Deadest dump in the country. Go on further south. That's where all the pyramids and Aztec temples and the other tourist attractions are."

"I think I'll just stay a few days and look around."

"You won't see anything. There's nothing here. But if you insist on sightseeing, I'll take you around. There's a couple of churches and that sort of crap. And maybe we can stop off in a cantina and have a few beers. This town's so sleepy it's a pleasure to run into a newcomer, believe me."

"No thanks," Alex said. "I'll just stroll about on my own."

The other took him by the arm and started heading in the direction Alex had been heading. "No trouble," he said. "I'm just killing time until I go on later at the hotel. Somebody said killing time isn't murder, it's suicide. But that's all there is to do in San Raphael."

Alex gently extracted his arm from the other's friendly grip. "No thanks," he said. "Actually, it's the way I like to discover a new place. Wander around by myself. Get the flavor. Where's the library?"

The other came to a halt and his thin face twisted into a scowl. "The what?"

"The library."

"What library? A Mexican pueblo this size never has a library. Most of these people can't read anything more advanced than a spick comic book."

Alex looked at him. "I got the impression that it

was kind of a foreign colony library, not Mexican. That girl that sat next to you, last night. Lilith told me she was the librarian. But never mind, I speak Spanish. I can ask one of these locals."

Jack Fast said quickly, "Oh, you mean the Biblioteca? Oh, sure. It's not a regular public library, like I thought you meant. I'll show you where it is. It's got an interesting Spanish Colonial facade. You'll like it. And right down the street a ways there's a native bar. Did you ever try pulque, the Mexican national drink? They make it from the maguey plant. Kind of like a cactus. If you're a stranger to Mexico, you'll want to try it."

"I'm not a stranger to Mexico," Alex said flatly. "And I've tried pulque. It tastes like vomit. Where's the Biblioteca? I'm interested in going in and browsing around a little, not just admiring the facade."

The other laughed lightly and made a gesture of apology. "Well, okay. I just thought I'd give a fellow American a steer. Just continue down Hidalgo, that street over there, to Calle Insurgentes. It's number 30. I'm not sure it's open this time of day. Have you seen the market? All sorts of handicrafts and the kind of souvenirs you might want to pick up for gifts back home."

Alex said, "Thanks, but I've seen a Mexican market. Why the hell don't you go back and tell Ursula I'm still out to see this town?"

Jack Fast looked at him in lack of comprehension and as though he was being put upon. "I don't know what you're talking about, friend."

"Okay," Alex said. "See you in the bar tonight. I

owe you a drink for going so far out of your way to help me."

He turned and headed for Calle Hidalgo, leaving the other behind. Damn it, he'd been too heavy-handed.

The facade of the Biblioteca was attractive at that. But the average passerby would have had no indication that it fronted for a library. There was no sign advertising the fact. There wasn't even a plaque giving the hours and days it was open. The doors were ajar but there was precious little traffic going in and out. Certainly not Mexicans. He stood there, across the street, for a few minutes looking at it and during that time just one person left, two books under his arm. It was obviously one of the foreign colony, a conservatively dressed elderly man.

Alex crossed the street and entered.

Once again, the building was a working over of what once must have been a Spanish Colonial mansion, or, just possibly, some sort of religious construction such as a monastery or orphanage. There was the inevitable large patio in the middle and the multitude of rooms of varying sizes opening off it. He got the impression that the library proper, the rooms crowded with book shelves, were probably the result of knocking down partitions and amalgamating two or three rooms, formerly living or bedrooms, to create more size.

Close by the door, under a portico, was what was obviously the librarian's desk. Behind it was seated—now what had Lilith said her name was? —Fay Morgan, the girl friend of Jack Fast. Or, at least, she had sat next to the pianist the night before and he had played for her what was obviously a favorite song, or possibly a standing joke between them.

He decided against Irish in favor of Welsh. Seen in the light of day, the striking brunette had an elfin quality about her. Alex wondered what she must have looked like as a teenager. Not that he didn't prefer the more mature woman she was now.

She looked up from her paperwork, a slight frown there. She obviously recognized him, strangers were a rarity in San Raphael and she would have noticed him sitting with Lilith the night before.

She said, her voice with the lilt of the Welsh in the background, "Could I do something for you?"

Alex smiled. "This is the library, isn't it? I'd like to look at a book."

She didn't follow along. "Do you have a card?"

He looked at her. "I've only been in town since noon, yesterday. How could I have a card?"

"I'm afraid you can't take out books without a card, sir."

He hid his exasperation. "How much is a library card?"

"Five hundred pesos."

"For a library card?"

"The library is self-supporting. Almost all of our books and periodicals are donations but there are other expenses. There are so few of us to support our Biblioteca that we have to charge rather high rates of the membership."

"All right," he said. "Today, I'll just look around. If I decide to stay in San Raphael I'll pony up the five hundred."

She hesitated. But then, "Oh, you won't want to stay in San Raphael. It's probably the most inhospitable town in Mexico."

"So I'm finding out."

"Oh, what I meant was that there is so little to do here. It's drab, dull . . ."

"So everybody, but everybody, tells me," he said, completely with sarcasm. "But I still think I'll give whatever is offered a look. Thanks."

He turned and headed for the first of the rooms boasting the usual book shelves to be found in libraries. She looked after him, her full bottom lip between her teeth.

The Biblioteca was, as Lilith mentioned the night before, on the different side. The few novels weren't quite as dated as she had led him to believe but damned near it. The thing was, for all practical purposes, there was no fiction. Certainly, not one tenth of the volumes represented were fiction, novels, drama, poetry, or otherwise. What there was was science with a vengeance.

He went down the long lines of book shelves. Biology in all its branches, genetics, gerontology, medicine, endocrinology, physics, cryonics, chemistry, even, of all things, such pseudosciences as alchemy and astrology. Even the social sciences were represented, though not as heavily as the hard ones.

From time to time he recognized a work. *Aging Life Processes*, edited by Seymour Bakerman; *Extended Youth*, by Prehoda; *Biological Mechanisms of Aging*, by Howard Curtis; *Pathways to the Decisive Extension of the Human Specific Lifespan*, by Johan Bjorksten; *No More Dying*, by Joel Kurtzman.

The volumes were classified largely by the science. They were in half a dozen or more languages, especially English, German, Russian and French but were not segregated on this basis. It was as though those in charge of the library assumed that the readers were multi-lingual and had command of the full range of tongues. In some respects, the Biblioteca was a museum of scientific works. The volumes ran in publication dates from the 18th Century to the current year. A few were even earlier. He would have thought some would have been preserved under lock and key, their value must have been astronomical.

Werner Gottlieb was represented half a dozen times including two volumes that Alex hadn't known existed. His eyes narrowed when he checked the publication dates, and the printer. Both books, in German, had been published in the small town of Hedge, near Heidelberg, in the year 1885. He put them carefully back on the shelves and continued his explorations.

There were interesting aspects. Despite the mustiness of the atmosphere in general, and the predominance of aged, foreign publications, the Encyclopedia Britannica was the latest edition! And so were such reference books as the *Harper Encyclopedia of Science*.

In the periodical room, he found that the library subscribed to half a dozen of the world's foremost newspapers, ranging from *The New York Times* to *Pravda*. Not to speak of such magazines as the *Journal of the American Gerontology Society*, a copy of which he had noticed in the Sierra Nevada bar the afternoon before. The periodicals, as the books, were in a wide range of languages, including Russian, and consisted exclusively of scientific journals.

Already, he had found what he was looking for.

He returned to the librarian's desk and said to Fay Morgan, "Do you have a telephone directory?"

She looked at him, as though disapprovingly and said, "There is no phone directory in San Raphael. You must realize that there aren't many phones. This isn't a very progressive town."

"I know. It's also dead, dull and atrophied. Or, as Jack Fast puts it in a bit of slang almost as aged as the tunes he plays, it's endsville. Do you have a telephone I could use?"

She hesitated for a moment but then pointed briefly and said, "In my office there. Not a long distance, I assume?"

"No, not a long distance. Thanks."

He crossed to the small office she had indicated. It held little more than a desk with an old fashioned electric typewriter, two steel files and two chairs, one of them a swivel type behind the desk. He sat down in it.

The telephone had no visual screen nor even punch buttons but rather the old dialing system. Next to it was a paperbacked booklet. It read, "CELAYA: Directorio Telefónico."

Unless he was mistaken, Celaya was the state capital. He took up the directory and opened it. Fully three quarters of the names and numbers of subscribers were in Celaya itself but following that city were a score of towns: Pozos, Roque, San Juan, San Felipe and, yes, San Raphael de Aldama. Most of the smaller villages boasted no more than a dozen or so subscribers apiece, but San Raphael was different. There were at least two hundred names.

He went over them carefully. Possibly fifteen were Mexican, or rather Spanish, names and he ignored them. The others were American or European other than Spanish. He ran a finger down the list and found six that he recognized: Cohen, David; Eden, Lilith; Fast, Jack; Fu, Hsu; Morgan, Fay; and Zavala, Ursula, whose number was the same as that of the Sierra Nevada. In actuality, what he was looking for were other names he recognized such as Werner Gottlieb. He found none save the six. For that matter, he didn't find Werner Gottlieb listed, either.

Momentarily, he sat there and stared down at the page. Then he went back over it more carefully and stopped when he reached Warner Goddard. He looked at that name for a long moment, then, on an impulse, pulled the phone over and dialed the number.

A feminine voice answered after three rings. "Bueno?"

Alex said, "¿El señor, por favor?"

"Uno momentito, por favor."

Shortly, another voice came on the line. "Ja?" it said.

It was the voice of Herr Professor Werner Gottlieb. Alex hung up.

He went back to the directory, got out a notepad and stylo and noted down the Goddard address, 17 Hospicio, and then reread the American and European names again. John Smith was there and

Thomas Jones. There were also Johan Schmidt and Jean Dusage and Hans Braun.

Alex Germain closed his eyes in pain. He muttered, "Oh, God, the babes in the woods. They're so naive as to hide by calling themselves such pseudonyms as John Smith."

3.

He put the phone book back in the exact place he had found it and got up and returned to the librarian's desk under the portico. He brought his wallet forth, selected a five hundred peso note and put it down before her.

"I'd like a membership card. I want to take out a couple of your books."

She blinked down at the banknote and then stared up at him, her lower lip in her faultless white teeth.

He looked at her politely.

She cleared her throat and said, "You have to be recommended by one of the other members."

He laughed, even as he picked up the high denomination bill again. "I wondered what you'd figure out," he told her.

She tried to look severe but there was the very smallest of twitches at the side of her mouth.

He said, "Are you a member?"

"Of course."

"Will you recommend me?"

"I don't even know you."

"My name is Alex Germain. Is Ursula Zavala a member?"

She hesitated for a fraction of a moment before saying, "No."

Which was, on the face of it, ridiculous. Any foreigner in a town with as little to offer in the way of activity and entertainment would belong to the library.

However, he said, "How about Professor Gottlieb? I notice a couple of his books are inside. Don't tell me he's not a member."

"I'm afraid I don't know any Professor Gottlieb." She was looking at him very unhappily.

"Try Warner Goddard."

"Señor Goddard is a member," she admitted.

Alex returned the bill to his wallet. He said, "Your name is listed in the Celaya phone book as Morgan, Fay. That wouldn't be Morgan le Fay, would it, sister of Arthur Pendragon?"

Her dark eyes widened in disbelief. "I don't know what you're talking about," she got out.

"Morgan le Fay," he said, smiling as though asking forgiveness. "Sometimes Morgain le Fay. Sorceress. Appeared sometimes, however, as a benevolent queen, sometimes identified as the Lady of the Lake. She gave Arthur Excalibur, his famous sword. She supposedly inhabited a castle in an underwater kingdom. According to one legend, she kidnapped the infant Launcelot and raised him until he grew to manhood."

She said impatiently, "I've read Tennyson's *Idylls of the King*."

"I'll bet you have."

She bent her head over the papers before her. "And now, if you'll excuse me."

But he noted that despite her dark cream complexion there was a slight flush at her neck.

He had thought of something and turned and went back into the library. He had his work cut out finding what he was looking for but finally did in a sudden inspiration in a small, very old looking book on Demonology.

He had been searching for the derivation of the name Dulcinea. It turned out that she was a succubus, the feminine counterpart of an incubus. It turned out also that succubi were demons who assumed the shapes of women and sought out men at night. St. Jerome had recorded his confrontation with the one named Dulcinea. She had already raised goosepimples on him—saint or nay—and he was about to take her when she suddenly escaped from his arms. Alex read further. Servius Tullius, one of the Etruscan reges of Roma, was the offspring of an incubus, according to the demonographers. That was interesting, Alex thought. It would seem the superstition involving incubi and succubi went back to before the Christian era. He had to chuckle at his memory of the night before. At least his visitor had a sense of humor, not to speak of a certain erudition, to call herself by that name.

Now that he was at it, another name occurred to him. Somewhat to his surprise, he found it in the same small volume. Lilith. According to Hebrew legend, Eve wasn't the first woman Jehova created. Lilith, revealed the Rabbinical literature, preceded her. The personality and name evidently derived from the Babylonian-Assyrian demon Lility or Lilu. The story was that she was the first wife of Adam but flew away from him to become a demon, and live forevermore.

He snorted even as he put the book back on the shelf. It was some name for parents to give a girl child. Lilith Eden's mother and father must have been atheists. Then it came to him. Lilith Eden. In other words, Lilith of Eden. He had a sneaking suspicion, not so sneaking, that the girl who looked like Nefertiti and who seemed to meet all newcomers to town and give them a negative rundown on San Raphael was operating under a pseudonym in the same manner that practically everyone else in the foreign colony was. At least, she seemed to have her tongue in cheek. It was better than, say, Jane Doe. But Lilith Eden, indeed!

As he left the Biblioteca, he winked at Fay Morgan, who was looking less than pleased. "Be seeing you," he said cheerfully.

She didn't answer.

Out on the street, he looked up and down undecidedly. Up Calle Insurgentes, to his left, he could make out the edge of the public market. As always, in Mexican towns, it overflowed from the building in which it was lodged onto the street.

As he had told Jack Fast, he had seen a Mexican market before. He turned and walked off in the other direction, his hands idly in his pockets, his pace a saunter. Alex Germain was projecting his easy-going self.

It came to him that the pueblo of San Raphael was spotlessly clean as Mexican small towns went. And there was a shortage of bedraggled, mangy, tail-between-the-legs dogs. Whoever heard of a Mexican village without a plentitude of disease

ridden pooches? Another thing came to him as he
passed a local policeman. The other was young,
alert looking and neatly uniformed in blue. He
was out of character in a Mexican village the size
of San Raphael. He should have been unshaven
and his uniform in need of a laundering at least a
couple of weeks before. And he should have been
belted with a monstrous horse pistol, looking as
though it was a rusty leftover from the civil war of
a few generations ago. This police officer carried a
small billy in a sheath at his side but no other
weapon.

Yes, San Raphael had its unique qualities.

Housing was thinning out now and he was about
to turn and retrace his way when he came to the
only really modern building he had thus far seen.
It was too spotless, too trim, to be anything except
what it obviously was, a hospital. And a hospital,
at that, of the quality to be expected of a town in
Texas or California thrice the size at least of this
Spanish Colonial pueblo.

A very well done gravel walk, flanked by lawn,
led up to the entry. Alex took it. The sign above the
door read simply "Clinica San Raphael de Aldama."
Before the door stood another of the clean cut
police officers. He eyed the newcomer but said
nothing as Alex approached and entered.

The lobby was standard, as hospitals went.
Largely white, spotlessly clean, obviously sterile,
the chairs, sofas and potted plants comfortable in
appearance and well done. To the right was a
reception desk and behind it two Mexican girls in
nurse uniform and looking trim and efficient, one

standing, one seated at a modern voco-typewriter making up some sort of a report.

The one standing smiled, took him in thoroughly with a quick glance and said, in English, "Could I help you?"

He said slowly, "Well, I'm new in town. Just looking around. I thought I'd sort of check out your facilities."

"Do you have a pass, sir?"

"A pass?"

"Yes, sir. It is forbidden that you go about the clinica without a pass."

From the side of his eyes Alex saw an elderly looking man in the white jacket affected by hospital personnel, including doctors, enter the room from one door and exit it through another, a clip board in one hand, an abstracted expression on his face. He looked Germanic, rather than Mexican.

"Where do I get a pass?" Alex said. "I'd just like to look around, uh, for future reference."

She twisted her lower lip regretfully. "Here," she said. "However, clinica regulations do not encourage visiting without cause."

He said, slightly exasperated, "You mean I need a pass to get into a hospital? Suppose I was sick. Maybe a rabid dog bit me on my way over here."

She awarded him an appreciative smile. "The emergency entrance is just around the corner to your left, sir. How do you know he was rabid? We are very careful with stray dogs in San Raphael."

He grinned back at her. "Actually, I was just curious. I've been wandering around town. It's a beautiful hospital. The government must be . . ."

"The Clinica San Raphael is privately endowed, sir."

"Oh, it is?" He let his eyes go about the lobby. "It's an impressive place. How many beds do you have?"

She answered before thinking over much. "Twelve."

He looked at her. "Twelve? In a building this size? No more than twelve?"

She said defensively, "San Raphael is a small town, sir."

"Then why would you need so much space for medical facilities?"

She was unhappy. "There are other things besides hospital rooms, that is, rooms for patients, in a clinica."

He nodded to that. "Yes, I imagine so. X-Ray rooms and all. I really don't know anything about it. Well, thanks."

He turned and left.

Outside, he looked back over his shoulder as he descended the walk. Twelve rooms? He would have guessed at least thirty by the size of the place.

He headed back for the town center, a dozen questions in his mind. Come to think of it, he had seen nobody in the building except the two reception girls and the doctor, or whatever he was, who had passed through the lobby. No patients, no visitors? What kind of hospital was it?

He wandered about a bit before finding what he sought. And, he might have guessed, it was located on the plaza, on the opposite side from the Parroquia church. As all the buildings on the Zócalo, it went back to Spanish Colonial times. There were several signs above it, of various sizes. They read,

Secretarian de Hacienda y Credito Publico, Secre-
taria de Finanzas, Tesorertia Municipal, and Presidente Municipal. In short, the one building which
would have been called the City Hall, in the States,
housed all town, State and Federal offices.

He didn't have nearly the difficulty in finding
what he was looking for as he had anticipated. A
one hundred peso propina to the sole clerk gave
him immediate assistance and access to the town's
current archives. His explanation was quite truthful.
He was looking up the ownership of a piece of
property in which he was interested.

There was a city chart, faithfully kept up to date
in a very neat, precise hand.

The Posada de Sierra Nevada, at Hospicio 15
was not owned by a Señora Ursula Zavala. Nor, as
he dug into the archives, had it ever been owned
by the Señora, nor ever by an Eduardo Zavala. It
was owned by a Señor David Cohen. His research
took him further. The hotel licenses, including the
liquor license, were held by a Señor Hsu Fu.

He found also that the beauteous Lilith Eden
had not been exaggerating when she had told him
in passing that between them Cohen and Hsu Fu
owned most of the town ruins of once magnificent
Spanish Colonial ruins. Most of the town, period,
belonged to one or the other of these two Mexicans
of Jewish and Chinese ancestry. For instance,
Hospicio 17, adjoining the Sierra Nevada and listed
in the phone book as the residence of Warner Goddard also belonged to Cohen. It took some thinking about.

A voice from behind him said in Spanish, "What
are you doing here?"

Alex turned. It was the Mexican Lilith had pointed out the night before as David Cohen.

He hadn't been able to make the man out very clearly in the dimness of the bar. Now he was somewhat surprised to find the other less Mexican and quite Semitic in facial appearance. In his time, Alex Germain had been in the Near East, including Yemen where perhaps resided the nearest thing to the Semitics of two thousand years ago to be found in the Arabian peninsula, including Palestine. Cohen did not have the Armenian nose, but then, contrary to some belief, most Semitics do not. However, he definitely looked like a Yemenite, small of build, delicate of features, kinky of hair, lithe of movement. Lilith had said, amusingly, that the original Cohen who came to Mexico at the time of the Conquest had not been able to find a nice Jewish girl as wife and had resorted to a nice Aztec girl. And, it was to be assumed, succeeding generations of Cohens had done the same. If so, why didn't the man look more Mexican, more Indian?

Alex said, also in Spanish, "I beg your pardon?"

The other now obviously recognized him and said, using English this time, "I am the presidente of San Raphael. What are you doing in this office?"

Alex turned on charm. "I'm batting around Mexico on sort of a vacation but at the same time I'm looking for a possible piece of property. Too young to retire, of course, but I thought I might buy a place to store my things, books and all, and come down a few months each year with the eventual view of retiring. I've been captivated by your town."

"Indeed," Cohen said. "And what property have you become interested in?"

The town chart was spread out on the table before him. Alex indicated with his forefinger. "That ruin immediately behind the Sierra Nevada. The terrace of my suite overlooks it. I though that with considerable reconstruction it would make an excellent investment."

"It belongs to me. It isn't for sale, I am afraid."

Alex looked at him. "Practically all property is for sale if the price is right."

Cohen eyed him up and down, taking in his clothes which were admittedly less than affluent in appearance.

"You are quite correct," he said, reversing himself. "The price is two million pesos."

Alex pretended to stare. "For that ruin! That's roughly $40,000 American. The property is actually not much more than an empty lot."

Cohen said evenly, "I have a great faith in San Raphael. I expect it to one day become an expensive resort. So I am holding on to my properties in expectation of eventually getting my prices for them."

Alex grunted rejection. "Well, I'm afraid you've priced yourself out of the market so far as I'm concerned."

"Indeed. Sorry. And now? I am afraid the clerk should have not allowed you in here without my permission. In the future, please let him look up any information you need from my offices."

"I didn't know the regulations," Alex told him. "I'll go. You don't know of any other properties that might be up for sale, do you?"

"No."

The younger man nodded and turned and left.

Out front of the municipal building he looked at his watch. Thus far, it had been an interesting morning. A little on the frustrating side, perhaps, but interesting. Now it was getting on towards lunch. He headed back in the direction of the Sierra Nevada, cutting across the Zócalo.

As he walked, he had the feeling of eyes upon him. Alex Germain believed in ESP—to a certain point. That is, he thought there was more to it than was commonly supposed by averagely intelligent people. In his experience he had run into events more than once that simply had no other answer. Telepathy, for instance, or even, which was more difficult for him to accept, an occasional flick of inspired intuition. And now he felt eyes upon his back. It wasn't just a girl who thought he was an attractive gringo, nor a pickpocket looking upon him as a potential mark. The eyes weren't particularly friendly nor unfriendly. Largely, they were just questioning. But very questioning. Somebody was very curious about Alex Germain.

He glanced about covertly but there must have been at least a hundred persons within sight. He couldn't imagine any of them with other than ordinary interest in him. As a stranger and a gringo, he expected some curiosity but not to this extent. He continued to feel the eyes until he reached Calle Correo. The pedestrian traffic thinned out there and he could have spotted anyone following him. But the feeling was gone. Was it of any importance? He shrugged.

When he arrived at the Sierra Nevada he hesitated and glanced at his watch again. Meal hours were later in Mexico, as late as in Spain. It wasn't at all unusual to have lunch at four o'clock and dinner as late as eleven or even midnight, especially among the upper class. And he'd had a late breakfast. In short, he still had some time on his hands before eating called.

He continued on beyond the small posada, which Nuscha called her own, and wasn't, to Number 17 Hospacio. The door as always in San Raphael was ornate. There was a large, heavy iron knocker. He banged with it.

A small, shy girl answered. She was very trim, very neat, but looked as though she couldn't be more than fifteen. Alex was amused by the snide suspicion that came to his mind. Was the celebrated scientist, Werner Gottlieb, inclined toward the Lolitas?

He said, "¿Señor Goddard, por favor?"

She said, "Uno momentito, Señor."

She let him into the entrada and left him there. It would seem that in the home of Herr Warner Goddard not even gringos were ushered in automatically. He looked about. The architecture was becoming familiar to him. Andalusian Spanish, combined with Moroccan with touches of Mexican Indian, particularly as it applied to flowers. There are always flowers in Mexico. The patio to which he could see on beyond, had attributes of the atriums in the Roman mansions of Pompeii. It had been a long time since he had been in Pompeii. How long? He couldn't remember.

Werner Gottlieb, alias Warner Goddard, came to greet him flanked by Buda who initially looked defensive but then gave his stub of a tail a grudging wag.

The Austrian scientist didn't offer his hand. He said stiffly, "I have been more or less expecting you."

Alex said, "Oh? Why, Professor?"

The older man sighed. "Because journalists are relentless. I suppose I must invite you in. The sooner all this is dispensed with the better. I am afraid that as the years pass I become less tolerant of intrusions upon my privacy." He turned and led the way through the patio to the living room. The girl had disappeared but Buda tagged along after giving the newcomer's pants leg a good sniff with his dark red nose.

Alex was a bit amused by the decor. Only lip service was paid to Mexico, a touch of color added in the hand woven rugs, a pre-Columbian pot centered in the central table. Otherwise, the room was one in which Goethe would have been comfortable, or perhaps Heine or Karl Marx, back in the early 19th Century, Teutonic and heavy in furniture and staid decorations.

Gottlieb motioned his unwanted visitor to a chair and seated himself across from him. The dog took his accustomed place at his master's feet, hung his tongue out in soft panting and kept his eyes on Alex.

Gottlieb said, with a sigh revealing he felt put upon, "You tell me you once covered a symposium of gerontologists which I presided over in Vienna."

"That's right, Herr Professor. It must have been a full twenty years ago. Excuse me, but I'm surprised to find you still alive."

The scientist ignored that. "If it is the same symposium I am thinking of, it must have been shortly after I received my Nobel. The notoriety disturbed me. I found it not conducive to the privacy I needed to work. Besides, as you say, I was getting along in years. Consequently, I, ah, retired and withdrew entirely from the University and my former colleagues. However, I was afraid that if I remained in Europe I would be continually sought out by journalists and others, particularly since at that time gerontology was so much in the news. That is why I came to this remote town in Mexico and, ah, changed my name. Now I can only request of you that you abide by an old man's heart-felt wishes and consider this interview, ah, off the record, I believe you newsmen call it. If you revealed my presence in San Raphael, I am afraid that I would again be badgered."

Alex nodded. "I can see your point, sir, and I promise not to publish anything that would reveal your presence here. However, in return, I'd expect to have you answer a few questions for me."

The other looked impatient but there was obviously nothing for it. He said, "Very well, but I do wish you would cut it short. Part of my health regimen involves a mid-day siesta."

"Okay, Professor. A moment ago you mentioned being an old man. Just how old?"

"I am afraid that is my business."

"Professor, in the Biblioteca I saw two of your books. They had been published in Germany in 1885, in short, over a century ago."

Gottlieb looked at him testily. "Good heavens, young man. They were written by my father whose name was also Werner. In the United States you would call me Junior."

Alex could only take that. He said, "Then he was a gerontologist too?"

"They didn't use that term in those days. However, yes. He was a pioneer in the field. And it is a field that I have pursued since youth. Undoubtedly, this accounts for your surprise at my years. I practice what I learned. The science, of course, is still in its infancy but already we are acquainted with methods to prolong life beyond the three score years and ten of the Bible."

Alex's eyes narrowed. "Such as what?"

"Various things. I could inform you right now on how to prolong your life at least ten years."

"Please do."

"Very well. If you smoke, stop. If you drink alcohol, do it moderately, perhaps an occasional beer or some wine. If you take any narcotics, even caffeine in coffee, tea or chocolate, stop. I, for instance, limit myself to an herb tea of this vicinity. You are already not a heavy-set man, but lose perhaps another ten pounds. Eat very lightly but nutritiously. Even though you are not a complete vegetarian, avoid much red meat. Prefer fish, especially sardines and salmon. Do not live in a large city. Live in an isolated place such as San Raphael where air and water are comparatively unpolluted. Exercise but not strenuously, perhaps two hours daily of walking. Above all, avoid stress. Do you remember a novel of some years ago entitled *Lost Horizon*, by James Hilton?"

"As a matter of fact, I do."

"Live like the monks in Shangri-La did. Do everything moderately, even sex. Never get upset about anything. Drop journalism as a profession, it involves too much stress. Do get married but to a quiet, easy-going woman who is approximately your own age and interested in the same things you are. Don't have children. Particularly in this age they cause stress. Never worry, about money or anything else." The professor twisted his mouth. "And, one other thing, don't ride in automobiles. Aside from the fact that they are one of the modern age's biggest killers, they cause stress."

Alex laughed in depreciation. "And if I could stick to all that, I'd live another ten years? Suppose I wanted to extend life another twenty years or more." He hesitated a moment, before adding, "As you seem to have done."

"Then daily take antioxidants Vitamin C, Vitamin E and the trace element selenium."

The journalist's eyes narrowed infinitesimally again. "And thirty?"

"Then you might look into the work of the late Dr. Anna Aslan, of Rumania. She investigated important antiaging results from injections of procaines along with B vitamins. The critical reason for the effectiveness of this therapy is that through a complex series of chemical reactions, five of the nine basic units of the purine molecule may be created. Purine plays a key role in creating nucleic acids and many important coenzymes. Also look into the work done in the Soviet Union with Vitamin B_{15}, that is, pangamic acid. Large daily injections of this vitamin are useful in treating various degenerative diseases including hardening of the arteries. Pangamic acid contains methyl groups which, along with folic acid, help create purines. Both B_{15} and procaine owe much of their effectiveness to their ability to put into motion bodily processes which create nucleic acids DNA and RNA both most necessary for prolongevity."

"You're getting out of my depth," Alex lied.

"I am afraid that there is nothing I can do about that," the Austrian scientist said. "And now if . . ."

"Just a moment, please," Alex said hurriedly. "When I met you, twenty-off years ago, you had just taken a Nobel prize in gerontology. There was a great deal of interest in the subject at the time. Overnight, it seemed to disappear. All of a sudden, the breakthroughs stopped. All of a sudden the predictions of prolongevity dried up. Why?"

Gottlieb sighed. "It is one of the reasons I dropped out. Funding of research was withheld. Governments stopped funding even research in geriatrics, usually to conserve the expenditures for military matters." He allowed himself a small sneer. "Science cannot operate without subsidy, not pure science. And it doesn't immediately pay off, as you Americans say. The major schools also cut back or completely eliminated research in gerontology when their budgets were reduced as a result of the Second Great Depression."

Alex pressed him. "But don't you believe that the people as a whole are still fascinated by the subject?"

Gottlieb sighed again and wearily as though looking forward to his nap. "I do not know of an age, nor a society, in which the people did not attempt to prolong life. Of all the life forms, man alone, it would seem, realizes the actuality of death. And in realizing it, attempts to avoid it. Usually, admittedly, he does this through religion. In all parts of the world we find the superstitious belief in an afterlife. Among the Christians and Moslems, though, surprisingly enough, not among the Jews, from whom their religions evolved, we have the conception of paradise in which, after leading an exemplary life, as demanded by their theologies, they find eternal happiness. As though happiness could be an eternal thing. Happiness, like sorrow, is a contrast and one cannot be experienced without the other. Perpetual happiness, like perpetual anguish, is ridiculous. It would seem doubtful that after burning in hell for a thousand years, it would any longer make much difference to the sufferer. So, it would seem, after a thousand years or so, the happiness of paradise would begin to pall. As Goethe put it, 'What is as boring as a succession of beautiful days?' "

Alex said, "Perhaps the pleasures of paradise and the anguishes of hell are different from those we enjoy, or suffer, on this, uh, earthly plane. Perhaps our souls are different from our material bodies. I would think they must be." He attempted a facetious note. "I cannot quite picture a youthful angel sitting on the edge of a celestial cloud masturbating."

The gerontologist scoffed. "I've run into that argument before. Let me tell you. When you say Werner Manfred Gottlieb, you say a man who enjoys good food, an occasional beer, frank sex, music, the companionship of compatible people and long intelligent conversations with them. A man who likes chess, hiking and mountain climbing.

A man who loathes politics and politicians, war and avarice, racism and nationalism. All these are just a few of the facets of Werner Gottlieb. If you take them away, any of them, you are no longer talking about Werner Gottlieb. If there is not good food, good beer, good sex, good lusty jokes, in heaven, then whatever goes there, a soul, or whatever, is not me. What it might be, I cannot say, but it will not be me. The love, or dislike, of those things are what make up Werner Gottlieb.''

''Well, I suppose that makes considerable sense,'' Alex conceded. ''But what else about this striving on the part of the human race for prolongevity?''

''My dear young man, the belief in a paradise is not the only answer to death that religion presents us with. Reincarnation, either in human bodies born in the future, or even into other life forms, is also advanced as a method of avoiding final death. Hundreds of millions, especially in the Orient, subscribe to the belief. But religion, in all its multitudinous forms, is not the only method man has devised to avoid the unavoidable. The seeking of the Elixir of Life during the Middle Ages was far from the first attempt to find a method of extending the life span indefinitely. All cultures have attempted it, in all ages, in all lands. Long before the alchemists, the Orientals, the Mesopotamian civilizations, the Egyptians, the Aztecs and Incas, sought methods to avoid the reaper.''

The elderly scientist twisted his face into a grimace. ''One of the most fascinating, I have always thought, was that proposed by the ancient Chinese Taoists who taught in the concept of hsien that man could live eternally by respiratory, dietary and spiritual techniques. But the most important were sexual techniques, especially the practice of coitus reservatus while one's lover was having orgasm. Supposedly, he who could carry out this act several tens of times in one day and night could be cured of all maladies and extend his life indefinitely. If he changed lovers several times a night it was still more effective and if he changed them ten times in one night, that was especially excellent."

Alex laughed. "Well, it would be somewhat frustrating trying out the theory. But anything for science." He hesitated for a moment then said, in a switch of subject, "Professor, it is still difficult for me to accept what must be your age. It . . ."

"Nonsense," the other scoffed. "Others, knowing much less about the subject than I do, knowing much less how to achieve prolongevity, have lived to ripe ages. Among the Greeks, Sophocles, the playwright, lived to 90 years and Isocrates, the orator to 98 years. Enrico Danolo, the 12th Century Doge of Venice, fought a major war against the Byzantines at 96 and was still Doge at 97. Titian, the Renaissance artist, was still painting at the age of 99. Bernard Le Bovier de Fontelle, the French writer, lived to be 100. More recently, Bernard Shaw was vigorous until death at 94, and Bertrand Russell was still active in his midnineties."

"I suppose there are many examples down through history," Alex agreed.

The Austrian scientist nodded definitely. "So far as we know, Shirali Mislimov of Azerbaidzhan, was the oldest person ever to live. He was born in

1805 and died in 1973. The Soviet government officially affirmed acceptance of his assertion to be 168 years of age. Katherine Plunket of England lived to be 112. The ex-slave Charlie Smith of America lived to be over 120. Miguel Carpio, one of a good many centenarians in Vilcabamba, Ecuador, lived to his early 130s but was eclipsed by his friend Jose David who died in 1973 at the age of 142. There are many other examples, Mr. Germain. It is not at all unique to reach an age of 100."

Alex came to his feet. "I've overstayed my welcome." He smiled. "If any."

He was about to make his thanks and leave but Buda stood up and approached and gave him the paw on one knee.

Gottlieb sighed and said, "He wants to be scratched. I've seldom seen him accept a stranger so quickly."

In his time, Alex Germain had had many a dog. He was a dog man and had little time for other pets such as cats, birds, or even for horses. He bent expertly and began to give the Hungarian hound the old one-two. Up and down the back, roughly, not gently. A dog-sized scratching, using both hands. Buda went into what was obviously agonizing ecstasy, his rear legs caving in until he was almost belly on the floor.

Alex laughed and gave him a final pull of the ears and headed for the door.

"I can find my way out," he said to his host.

Buda looked after him wistfully, panting slightly, his long red tongue hanging out. "Thanks," he said.

Interlude

He sat in a comfortable chair and stared up for a few minutes. He shook his head and sighed, even as he activated his small transceiver. Somewhere up there was an unmanned satellite which was about to receive a message from him and then relay it to another person halfway around the globe. Time marches on, good Lord, but time marches on.

With his stylo he punched out the necessary code. In only seconds a face faded in.

"Hi, Magdalene," he said.

She was a plain looking, earnest looking young woman, done up no-nonsense wise, her hair, for instance, in a tight bun behind her head. But on his appearance her eyes went soft, becoming almost attractive.

"Well, hello," she said. "I must say, it's been donkey's years."

"Yes, and I'm sorry. I meant to look you up the last time I was in London. It just didn't work out."

"Mind that it does the next occasion, Monsieur."

"Rebuke accepted. Listen, Maggie, I want to check out the Dossiers Complete of several characters."

"I say, you know I'm not allowed to do that."

"I know." He hesitated. "It's very important to me, Maggie."

"They'd boot my bum out of this job so quickly." She looked her disgust. "I should never have let you do such a favor for me."

"But you did, Maggie," he said softly. "And now I'm afraid I'm calling in the account."

She took a deep breath. "Very well, what do you wish?"

"First, the dossier of David Cohen, who lives here in San Raphael de Aldama, Mexico."

"Righto. Hang on. Smoke a cigarette or something."

"What, and get lung cancer?"

She came back in a surprisingly short time. "All right, what did you want, ducky? There's surprisingly little. The *Dossiers Complete* of Europeans, Americans, Japanese and so forth can be quite complete indeed, however, the developing countries don't cooperate to the same extent."

"A general rundown."

"One of the oldest Mexican families and one of the most wealthy. Fortune based on the silver of Guanajuato running back to the Spanish Conquest. No marriage. No children. This doesn't seem likely but no education. He's currently presidente, that is, mayor, of San Raphael but the family never seems to have participated in Mexican politics on a national or even statewide basis, which, if I'm not mistaken, is somewhat unique in Mexico."

"What was his father's name?"

"David Cohen and his grandfather's as well. The name is the same all the way back to the Conquistadores."

"Mother's name?"

"No record. Nor grandmother's either. You'd think the whole line was composed of illegitimate births. Nor can I find any record of other relatives. But, of course, these are Mexican files. They're very inadequate, don't you know. But no brothers, sisters, no anything save David Cohen all the way back to the 1500s.''

"Holy smog," he said. "What else is there about him?"

"Practically nothing. His dossier is abnormally incomplete. My guess would be this would have to be deliberate. He has undoubtedly pulled strings. Strings are pulled more easily in smaller countries.''

"All right. This next one will be more productive. Werner Gottlieb, of Austria, the celebrated gerontologist and Nobel laureate.''

"Oh, I've heard of him, ducky. Half a mo'.''

She was back in not much more than half a minute, at that, but her face expressed disbelief.

She said, "I don't know what you're looking for but all the records of his early life were lost in the bombing of Dresden in the Hitler war. Of course, there's a great deal about his work and his published things. Did you want that?"

"No. I've read most of them. When was he born?"

"There's no information on that.''

He stared at her. "Look, the man is . . .''

"Was.''

". . . a Nobel prize winner. Even if his early history was destroyed he would have reconstructed it for his biographers and, well, for all the interviews and . . . What do you mean was?"

"He died eighteen years ago, dear. He was very old, you know.''

"Where? How? Do you have any of the obits?"

"There's practically nothing in the obituaries save on his work. He died of heart failure in Izamal, Yucatan, Mexico. By Mexican law, probably going back to the days before refrigeration, a corpse has to be buried within twenty-four hours. He was buried before any reporters could have gotten to Izmal."

"I'll be damned. Listen, look up Warner Goddard, presently residing in San Raphael de Aldama, Mexico."

Time passed but she said finally, "There is nothing in the International Dossier Banks on a Warner Goddard, Ducky. Which is rather strange, if he exists."

He hissed air out of his lungs. "All right. How about a Hsu Fu, also of San Raphael?"

"How do you spell it?"

"It's Chinese. H-s-u F-u."

It took her longer this time. She came back on, looking more mystified than ever. "There is no record of a present day Hsu Fu."

"What do you mean, present day? What kind of record do you have?"

"Well, actually, ducky, it's more legend than anything else. According to the Shih Chi, the earliest of the Chinese dynastic histories, finished in the first century, B.C., there were supposed to be three blessed isles situated in the Eastern Ocean. Many immortals inhabited them since there was a drug that would prevent death there. The Emperor Chin Shih Huang Ti commissioned an expedition in 219 B.C. headed by a Hsu Fu to seek out the islands. According to the Shih Chi, Hsu Fu found them but the sea mage in command told him scornfully that the presents he had brought were insufficient for the drugs which promoted longevity. Hsu Fu returned to the emperor who provided him with a larger expedition. The Shih

Chi account winds up saying that Hsu Fu never returned to China."

"Sounds like one of the original con games," he growled. "Look. Just one more. This might take longer, in which case I'll call you back tomorrow."

She sighed, "All right, ducky."

"The name is Ahasuerus. When last heard about, so far as I know, he was in Seville, Spain in the 16th Century."

"Good grief, dear. How do you spell the name?"

"A-h-a-s-u-e-r-u-s. It's a Hebrew name, going way back. There's more about him in the old archives than you might think."

She said doubtfully, "Well, I'll try but not even we have much information on obscure Hebrews in Spain in the 16th Century."

"Look him up under The Wandering Jew."

Chapter 3

Because biological immortality and the pres-
ervation of youth are such potent lures, men
will never cease to search for them, tanta-
lized by the examples of creatures who lived
for centuries and undeterred by the unfortunate experience of Dr. Faust. It would be fool-
ish to imagine that this search will never be
successful, down all the ages that lie ahead.
Whether success would be desirable is quite
another matter.
—Arthur C. Clarke
Profiles of the Future

1.

Somewhat bemused, Alex Germain entered the
patio of the Sierra Nevada. Momentarily, he looked
in the direction of the bar but then rejected it. He
was in no position to repeat the day before and

slop down more booze than this altitude allowed him. Instead, he headed for the dining room.

Ursula Zavala, harried looking as usual, emerged from the office heading in the same direction.

The tall blonde saw him and said tartly, "Hello, Alex. Did you see San Raphael? And how did you find it?"

He ran a hand through his short cut hair and looked rueful. "Beyond my expectations," he told her. "But it wasn't San Raphael that got me down. It was the chat I just had with Gottlieb . . . and Buda."

The Teutonic blue eyes took him in sarcastically. She said, "I know, I know. You did something, such as scratching the dog, and he said, 'Thanks.'"

He stared at her. "How did you know?"

"It's his party trick. I assume it's taken Werner years to teach him. Those two old bachelors live together like man and wife. Even closer. They're never outside each other's sight."

"Listen, dogs don't have a voice box."

"Neither do cats. However, I once had a friend who claimed her cat could say his own name. And he could. It was Raoul. Buda's vocabulary is admittedly limited but Werner has persevered and amuses himself by startling people who don't expect his dog to be able to thank them."

Alex looked disgusted. "I was half expecting him to show off by delivering Hamlet's soliloquy."

She was half turning to go on her way when he said, "When do you eat, Nuscha?"

She said flippantly, "On the fly. It's according to how busy we are."

"How about lighting long enough, in your flight,

to have lunch with me? I wanted to ask you a few things."

She looked at him warily but then her eyes shifted and she said, "All right. I can have Marcelo set up a table out here in the patio where I can keep an eye on things as we eat."

"Holy smog," he said. "Don't you get ulcers?"

"I haven't had time," she told him and then called through the door to the dining room for her maitre d'.

There was a small table a dozen feet or so from the entry to the office and an equal distance from the dining room door. They sat at it in comfortable wicker chairs while Marcelo and one of the waiters brought table cloth, napkins and the other requirements.

Ursula ordered a bottle of Chinon Blanc.

To keep in character, Alex said, after the waiter had departed, "Hey, I can't afford the prices you charge for wine here."

"It's on the house," she told him. "What were you chatting over with the professor?"

He made a wobbly motion with his right hand. "Oh, odds and ends." He risked a gamble. "You know, thinking back, that's the same dog he had there in Vienna."

She seemed to freeze momentarily, then caught herself. "You mean Buda? He's a Vizsla. Werner always has Vizslas, one after the other. They all look alike. They've been interbred for centuries. It's impossible to tell one from another."

"Yes, but the one he had in Vienna was named Buda too."

She said, too quickly, "He names them all Buda."

And then she came to a stop and paused a moment before saying, "You couldn't have seen Werner's dog in Vienna. You met him in my pension. But dogs aren't allowed in restaurants and bars in Austria, so when Werner came there to play chess with his cronies and colleagues Buda had to be left at home."

He grinned at her. "Testing, testing . . ."

She wasn't amused and she obviously didn't quite understand what he was trying to do. Frowning, she fiddled with her overgrown earring.

Marcelo came with their wine and the menus.

When he was gone again, Ursula said, "You didn't answer my question. What did you talk about with Werner?"

"He was trying to keep me from mentioning in any of my articles the fact that he had gone to ground here in San Raphael. I said okay if he'd answer a few questions. And he gave me a lot of gobbledygook as answers to them."

She looked at him. "That doesn't sound like the professor. What kind of gobbledygook?"

"I brought up the fact that he was obviously more than ordinarily aged. He brushed that aside and pointed out that as a gerontologist he practiced what he taught. That if I took Vitamins C and E and selenium I could add possibly twenty years to my life due to their antioxidant qualities."

She frowned again. "He should know. He's a Nobel laureate in the field."

Alex said sourly, "So was Linus Pauling and as far back as 1978 at a Palm Springs conference he said that if you'd take 10 grams of Vitamin C every day you'd live sixteen years longer. The trouble is, he failed to provide any evidence to back up the claim. Since then, Harold Massie fed fruit flies, who, like us, do not make their own Vitamin C, large amounts of the stuff. He found that the high intake of C shortened their life span up to almost 13 percent. The higher the dosage, the more the shortening. Small amounts had no appreciable effect. Then Davies and Hughes fed guinea pigs large amounts of Vitamin C, starting at five weeks of age. Once again there was a shortening of life span. In fact, there were a significant number of early deaths associated with a high level of ascorbic acid consumption. I could give similar examples of experiments with Vitamin E. It went through quite a fad for a while but none of the experiments supported the claim that it extended life span. Same with selenium, one of the trace elements. Both it and C might have beneficial effect on cancer but there's no evidence it prolongs life. In spite of all the ballyhoo over Vitamins E and C, pantothenic acid, one of the B complex, is the only vitamin that has been shown to prolong life span in mammals. It's the primary nutritional constituent in royal jelly, which fed to female bees turns them into queen bees which live for six to eight years, rather then the one month of the usual female bee. Gardner fed the vitamin to fruit flies and found it extended their life spans too. And in 1958 Pelton and Williams experimented with it on black mice. They increased the life span 19 percent."

Marcelo came up with pad and pencil and took their orders. Ursula had a salad of the house and Alex settled for fish in garlic and a green tossed salad after finding from his companion that she had the seafood brought in from the coast twice a week.

When the waiter had gone again, Ursula scowled and said, "What else?"

He gave a little shrug. "When I continued to dwell on his own obviously advanced years, he gave me a lot of double-talk about the numerous individuals who had lived beyond a century. You know, the old wheezes about Vilcabamba, Ecuador, the Hunza valley in Pakistan, and especially the Caucasian mountain region of Georgia in the USSR. He even drug up Muslimou of the Soviet Republic of Azerbaijan, who supposedly lived to be 168 years of age."

"I've heard about him," Ursula protested. "What are you sneering about?"

"It was nonsense. There is no authentication. In Georgia, in the old days, many men took the names of their fathers to avoid military service in both the World Wars. The practice was particularly prevalent in that part of the country. When Stalin, who was a Georgian himself, took a personal interest in the centenarian reports as he grew older, the claims were officially endorsed by the government. And as the local officials promoted the sensational claims, to please Stalin, the oldsters began to enjoy the attention they were getting. Years later when investigators, supposedly serious scientists, showed up from Europe and the United States, there wasn't much trouble pulling the wool over their eyes. The Georgians had been lying about their ages for the better part of a century. They had the time of their lives. One American TV crew even came and had the supposed one hundred years plus citizens demonstrating eating yogurt, an ad for an American yogurt company that wanted to put over how healthy their product was. How much they tipped their amateur actors is up for grabs."

"That wouldn't apply to Vilcabamba and the Hunza valley."

He was irritated and after their food had been served them, said, "Come on, Nuscha. What kind of records do you think they have in Pakistan and the interior of Ecuador? Birth certificates? A couple of decades ago Mazess and Forman got fed up with all the silly reports coming out of Vilcabamba and went down and in cooperation with Ecuadorian scientists conducted a census in the village, including about 850 of its thousand citizens. They reconstructed the family genealogies, matching them against civil and church records. One thing they found was that there were only a few given names, invariably those of saints such as Juan, Diego and Jose. You'd have the same names in a family going back for centuries. At any rate, they came up with the proof that the average so-called centenarian was about eighty-six and the oldest person in town was ninety-six. It was found that the pattern of exaggeration usually began at about the age of seventy and amounted to as much as twenty to forty years. Sure, they found more citizens over age sixty in Vilcabamba than the average in Ecuador but that was largely the result of the fact that younger persons left the village for larger towns to find jobs, rather than any apparent longevity factor."

He lifted a fork of the fish before continuing the attack.

"The *Guiness Book of World Records* lists a Canadian, Pierre Joubert, as the oldest person in history for whom there is authentication. He died at 113 plus 124 days. It lists only nine persons who have been authenticated as having lived for more than 110 years. The oldest American to have lived with adequate records to prove it was Fanny Leors Thomas, who died in January of 1981 also at the age of 113. By the way, she attributed her longevity to eating applesauce three times a day and to staying single."

She speared a shrimp from her salad and said accusingly, "You certainly seem up on the subject, quoting names, dates, statistics."

He said in annoyance, "Nuscha, I'm a freelance writer. Part of the game is to have a couple of fields in which you're knowledgeable. One guy will specialize in space travel, another in military subjects, another in vintage wines. I don't know anything about any of those. One of my specialties is gerontology. That's how come I got the assignment to cover that symposium Gottlieb presided over in Vienna. There isn't as much interest in the field as there used to be and probably for good reason. I find I seem always to come out the same door I went in."

"How do you mean?" For some reason they both seemed to have become irritated.

"If Gottlieb knew how to prolong life ten, twenty or thirty years, why hasn't he come out with the information? It'd make him the greatest scientist of the century."

She said tartly, "Perhaps he is aware of some of the ramifications."

"What ramifications? The world would make a hero out of him if he showed us how to prolong life even ten years, not to speak of thirty."

Her eyes glinted. "Are you so sure? Take just one aspect. What would happen to Social Security, military pensions, Civil Service pensions, and for all practical purposes all other pensions? Social Security was originally set up based on the fact that the average person would retire at age 65 and then live to the age of approximately 75, collecting benefits. Sure, some died at age 66 and lost out on the amount they had contributed, but some lived on to 85 or even a bit more and the investment of the deductions from their pay they had made over the years paid off nicely. But on an average the retired worker lived ten years and until he was about 75."

Marcelo, who had been hovering not too far off, came over and poured them more of the white wine. He looked a bit worried, for some reason or other, not quite the imperturbable perfect waiter he usually portrayed.

Alex said, "Go on."

She said, "All right, suppose that Werner released his information on how to add years to everybody's life span. Overnight, instead of dying at average age 75, the recipients of Social Security benefits would live to 85. What would happen to the Social Security administration? It's in enough trouble already, trying to pay off. What would happen to the Veterans' Administration? As it is, a person in the military can retire after twenty years of service and receive his pension for the rest of his life. Suppose he lived to be a century, rather than the present average of 75? How could the government continue to pay off? There are millions of vets."

Alex said, "They'd figure out something. People would rather live the extra decades than collect the pensions."

"Are you so sure? Why should a life span of 100 or more be preferable to one of 75 years? More of the same isn't necessarily a very good argument. Do you contend that the Beethoven sonatas or Shakespeare's plays are the less because they come to an end? If you can lead a full and satisfactory life in 75 years, why add a few decades? By the way, how would those extra thirty years be attached to the life span? Would childhood last an extra ten years, the prime adult years another ten, and then old age an extra ten? How would you like to change diapers an extra ten years? Or suppose you tacked on the entire thirty years to the end of life. How would you like to pay alimony for an extra thirty years?"

Alex had to laugh at her vehemence.

She said testily, "Three score years and ten are plenty. In fact, possibly a little too damn much. After you've experienced all the things you really wanted to do, a successful career in a field you liked, travel, sex, good food and so forth, why repeat it over and over? If you eat one gourmet meal, great. If you eat a couple of thousand, possibly great. But who wants to eat a million gourmet meals? The same with travel. There comes a point where travel palls. You can only see the Acropolis a few times and it's stale, or the Grand Canyon, or the Taj Mahal. After you've seen all the important things to see, then the devil with it. Intellectual pursuits? Even the keenest mathematician sooner or later gets tired of numbers and symbols. Look at Newton. He did all his important work as a young man and fizzled out in his middle years.''

Marcelo came up and said, "Señora, the telephone.''

She looked up at him, scowling, but then her face cleared and she blinked. She tossed her napkin to the table and stood.

"See you later, Alex," she told him and strode off energetically for the office.

Alex was through with the excellent fish he had ordered and put down his napkin. He said to Marcelo, "I'll sign for the bill." And, still keeping in character, added, "Señora Zavala said the wine was on her.''

"Very good, sir," Marcelo said and went for the check.

Alex looked after him thoughtfully.

Of a sudden he was tired. Partially, probably because of his long walk about town, partially his lack of sleep the night before, not so speak of his romantic gymnastics. He remembered again the fact that the altitude, more than a mile, took getting acclimated to. At the end of the week you were able to exercise your usual amount without becoming winded. And you could also drink as much as your usual quota. But it took a week or ten days.

After he had signed his bill he headed back for his room decided on a siesta. Midday naps weren't usually in his schedule but these circumstances called for one. As he passed the dining room he noted the two Texans, looking lonely and glum. Otherwise, there were half a dozen or so of the elderly foreign colony. In the light of day he could make them out better than he had in the dimness of the bar the night before and they still bore out what he had noticed. None of the men showed signs of baldness, nor did any of them wear glasses, nor, so far as he could see, hearing aids.

In his room, he kicked off his shoes and stretched out, his hands behind his head, and stared up at the ceiling. He had the feeling that there had been no phone call for Nuscha. That Marcelo had used the pretense to shut her up. And just who was the head waiter to monitor his boss's conversation and then censor it?

2.

Alex Germain had planned on an hour's nap but when he awoke it was to find that it was dark out. He went into the bath and sloshed cold water onto his face before looking at his watch. He was astonished. He had slept a good nine hours. Evidently, everything had caught up with him: the tiresome traveling on second class buses, the drinks of the day before, the sexual bout with Dulcinea, the long walk about the cobblestoned streets of San Raphael.

He went back into the bedroom and sat on the edge of the bed recapitulating. San Raphael and its inhabitants had their fascinating aspects. The windows that opened onto the patio were open and through them he could hear the tinkle of Jack Fast's piano. He was playing "For Me and My Gal." Alex grunted. The other's repertoire of the tunes of yesteryear seemed endless.

There was enough light reflected from the patio below to allow him to operate without turning on the room's illumination. He went over to his piece of luggage and brought it back to the bed and opened it.

He brought forth a pair of dark pants and a black turtlenecked sweater and redressed himself, then brought out a pair of black dress shoes and donned them. A black French beret and a black silk handkerchief he stuffed into his pockets. He went over and got the case containing his voco-typer, put it on the bed beside the suitcase and opened it and fished out a cloth sack with a draw string that obviously contained such items as spare ribbons, an oil can, cleaning brushes and some simple tools for emergency repairs. It contained a few other things too and he pocketed them. He closed both the suitcase and typewriter case and returned them to their place against the wall.

He went over to a window and looked in the direction of the bar. Only one of the tables before its entrance was occupied. It looked like the Beaumonts. He wondered why they remained in the town that had so obviously rejected them. The piano was playing "My Blue Heaven" and some-body was rendering the words. Probably Jack Fast he decided. He also decided that to render meant to tear apart. The voice wasn't exactly that of Bing Crosby or any of the other old timers who once sang "My Blue Heaven."

He turned and made his way out onto the terrace and for a moment went to its rear and stared thoughtfully down into the patio of the ruined mansion. There was an aged mesquite tree about four feet from the stone wall of the Sierra Nevada. It must have been at least a couple of centuries in age, he decided. The mesquite is one of the slowest growing trees in North America.

He turned and headed for the circular iron stairway that led to the roof of the hotel. He fished the beret from his pocket and pulled it over his blond hair before peering over the edge of the roof. There was nobody in sight. He hadn't expected there to be.

He began retracing the way he had taken that morning, heading for the stairway that led down into the main section of the building devoted to guest rooms. From the side of his eyes he saw a slight movement and froze. It had come from the adjoining building.

Alex peered into the darkness. And, yes, there in the shadows, in the same spot he had occupied this morning, lay Buda. The dog was watching him, as though interestedly.

Alex nodded. It was obvious the Vizsla was put out at nights. These Spanish Colonial Mexican houses were built like fortresses, so far as street entrances were concerned. About the only manner in which a sneak thief could enter would be by the way of the rooftops. The houses were constructed side by side for the full length of the street and a burglar need only gain access to the roof, possibly through one of the unoccupied ruins, and he would be able to go from one rooftop to the other until he reached his destination. Gottlieb played it safe. Other than perhaps a Doberman pinscher, Alex couldn't off-hand think of a dog more suited for guarding than a Vizsla, as the professor had said, once the war dog of the barbaric Magyars.

He proceeded on his way. On the stairs, before reaching the level of the corridor, he paused and listened. And could hear nothing. He went on down. There was no one in the hall. He reached out and flicked off the light switch on the wall. No light came from beneath any of the doors. He went down the hall stealthily, putting his ear to each door in turn. He could hear nothing. He suspected that the two Texans were the only hotel guests besides himself and they were below at the bar.

He wound up at the door he had found locked that morning, the one that looked as though it might be that of a broom closet. He brought a gadget from his right pants pocket and inserted it in the lock and fiddled for a moment expertly. He felt the tumblers turn and tried the doorknob. The door opened.

The room beyond was, of course, pitch dark. Alex slid inside and closed the door behind him. He brought forth a pencil sized flashlight and activated it. With the thin beam of light he swept the room. It was, as he had suspected, a very small chamber and without a window. Possibly in the old days, before the building had been converted into a hotel, it had housed a maid or other servant. Or perhaps it had been utilized only for storage. He located the light switch and flicked it on.

The room was sparsely furnished with a desk, two battered straight chairs, an aged four-drawer steel file and what looked like a white medical chest. He put his picklock and flashlight back into his pockets and stepped over to the desk. He sat down behind it and began going through the drawers.

He found blank passports of Mexico, the United States, the United Kingdom, France, Switzerland, the USSR, the People's Republic of China, Italy, Sweden and Spain. He found blank driver's licenses of the same nations and International Driver's Licenses as well. He found American Social Security cards and International Health Certificates. There were also represented a score of others of the various papers involved in establishing a false identity on an international basis. In one drawer he found dozens of visa stamps of the countries represented by the blank passports. There were also blank birth certificates, he noted.

And there was the rest of the paraphernalia of the forger. The pens, the various colored inks, the stamps, the ink pads. Alex Germain snorted wry amusement. In his time he could have used this equipment.

He took only moments to check out the steel file and the medicine chest. They contained nothing save official government releases and pamphlets dealing with the legal requirements involving passports and other papers of the countries represented in the desk.

Taking extreme care to leave no sign that he had been present, he closed the drawers and returned to the door and put out the light. For a moment he held his ear to the door and then opened it and moved quickly out into the hall. He turned, brought his picklock from his pocket and relocked the room before hurrying down the hall to the stairs where he flicked the hall's lights back on.

He hurried back up the stairs to the roof, crossed it, noting that Buda still held sentry duty, and descended the circular stairway to his terrace.

For a time he slumped down into one of the porch chairs there and recapitulated again. He wasn't as surprised as all that by what he had found although he was a bit by the fact that the plant was here in the Sierra Nevada. He would have expected it to be in some less vulnerable location, possibly in Cohen's home or that of Hsu Fu. But, why not? It became increasingly obvious that this hotel-pasada-inn was no more than a front. He suspected that long months could go by without any outsiders at all. Right now, there were the two Texans and himself. He suspected that Nuscha was seldom burdened with even that many outsiders at once. He stood again. He might as well be about it.

He went to the back wall and opposite the mesquite tree in the ruin beyond which David Cohen had coolly told him was priced at two million pesos. Two million pesos! By ordinary Mexican standards you should have been able to buy the Sierra Nevada for that much money, in this remote pueblo.

He swung his legs over the side of the parapet and pressed his feet against the bole of the tree and then, his back against the stone wall of the Sierra Nevada, began walking down, as a practiced mountain climber descends a rock chimney. When he reached the ground he headed for the front of the ruin. There was no door to the street, only the wreckage of one. He stepped out on the Calle Correo and looked up and down.

As he had expected, the streets of San Raphael were pulled in shortly after sunset. There was nothing to do, nowhere to go, especially for the natives, who certainly couldn't afford the bar or dining room of the Sierra Nevada. Up the street possibly three blocks he could see a sole pedestrian, by the looks of him slightly the worse for wear as a result of a tequila or two too many. He was staggering along undoubtedly heading for home after his cantina or pulqueria had closed its doors.

Alex Germain turned to the left and made his way in the direction of the Zócalo, keeping in the shadows. The town plaza was also deserted and he crossed in under the shade of the trees unobserved, at least so far as he knew. Not that it made much difference. There was no reason why he shouldn't be taking a stroll at this time of night. He was, after all, a gringo tourist presumably without the sense to be back at the hotel doing whatever it was that gringo tourists did at night.

Remembering his way, he went down two blocks of Calle Hidalgo to Insurgentes and the vicinity of the Biblioteca and then turned left and headed for the outskirts of the town.

He had no difficulty locating the "Clinica de San Raphael". At this time of night it wasn't overly illuminated. The reception room, yes. There was one light at the desk. And, even from across the street, he could see a nurse uniformed girl there. There was also dim light at a few of the windows, obviously coming through rather heavy drapes. One didn't get the feeling that there were too many in patients occupying the hospital.

He didn't approach from the front but circled the building, keeping to the shadows across the street. He was trusting that his black clothing made him all but invisible. In the rear, he spent a time motionless behind a tree carefully checking out the vicinity. He could see no one, either on the streets or near the building. He brought forth his black silk handkerchief and tied it about his face as a mask.

He crossed the street quickly and made it to the shelter of the dark, looming building. There were windows and one door of heavy glass. The windows were iron barred. Alex examined the door. It was locked. The picklock availed him nothing. There were undoubtedly bolts on the other side. No light came through the glass, so most likely this part of the building was unoccupied at this time of night.

Alex brought forth a burglar's glass cutter and cut out a triangle large enough for him to insert his hand. A bit of fumbling around and he was able to locate and throw the bolts. There were two of them.

He entered the door and closed it behind him. The corridor which stretched ahead was dark. He brought forth his tiny flashlight and used it sparingly to seek out his way. He had no real idea of what he was looking for.

He came to a white door and put his ear against it. Nothing. He carefully opened it. Dark inside. He flashed the light about. The room was a laboratory with scores upon scores of cages containing mice, rats and hamsters. Some of them squealed and scurried around at the intrusion.

He nodded to himself, closed the door behind

him and resumed his way down the corridor. The next room was obviously devoted to dissection. Half a dozen laboratory tables, microscopes, test tubes, Bunsen burners, all the paraphernalia associated with performing autopsies on small animals. He nodded again and went on.

The next room was locked and he didn't take the time to open it but pressed ahead. The following room was another devoted to cages with animals. In this case, tubs of fish as well as the more standard rats and mice in their cages. There were even two chimpanzees, who blinked into his light nervously and stirred about. He quickly reversed himself. All he needed was for the apes to raise a ruckus and have someone come to check them out.

He resumed his stealthy progress down the hall. Somewhere in here he suspected there would be an office. An office divorced from the hospital proper and devoted to the work going on in the laboratories. And half an hour in such an office would give him all he sought.

To his shock, a door suddenly opened and blinding light flared forth. A man in a white smock, a sheaf of papers in his right hand, issued forth. He was no more than fifteen feet from the black clad intruder.

Alex recognized him immediately. The aged Hsu Fu, the Chinese owner of half San Raphael, of whom there was no record. His first reaction was to turn and run for it. His black beret, his black silk mask, guarded him from being recognized.

But the other was on to him! The wiry, elderly Chinese dropped his sheaf of papers, screamed, "Sut!" at the top of his voice and lashed out with his right foot, in a typical Kenpo kick for the groin.

Alex dropped his flashlight and stepped back in alarm. The other was fast as a viper. With the edge of his left hand, Alex struck down at the other's ankle, diverting the vicious kick.

Hsu Fu screamed, "Sut!" again and bore in to the attack. He again kicked for the groin, missing, but simultaneously his right arm shot out straight as he swept the edge of his right hand in a whipping manner to the larynx of his opponent. The blow connected but only glancingly and Alex staggered back.

Alex tried to go into the 6th Kata as the terrible old man began a right-handed punch, Okinawa style. Alex moved in quickly, attempting, in his turn, a groin kick and flubbing it. Simultaneously, he raised his right hand shoulder high and shot it forward hard to the other's face, attempting with a finger-hand type blow to get at the Chinese combatant's eyes with his forefingers. But Hsu Fu moved his head quickly out of the way.

Alex Germain was under no illusions. The other was obviously an adept at Chinese Kenpo and probably Indian Nanpa Ken as well. It was seemingly impossible that the old man could fight like this. He was as strong and wiry as a pro.

He felt a blow he hadn't seen coming and reeled, the old man after him, again shouting his kiai yell. Alex felt, with agony, a chop to his right kidney and reeled back again.

He stumbled up against the door, the door through which the other had just emerged to discover him. Weakly, he slammed it shut, leaving them both in complete darkness.

As quietly as possible he sidestepped and sidestepped again. He could hear the other breathing deeply, but not so deeply as all that. Hsu Fu, in spite of the pace of the past few minutes, indicated no signs of exhaustion.

Alex Germain had no doubts. He knew very well that the Chinese could kill him with his hands. Kenpo is not a sport. It is a method, come down through the ages, of killing with the hands and feet. It was the ancestor of Karate, of Japanese Jujitsus and of Mongolian Hoppa Ken. Alex himself was no amateur in hand to hand combat but he was under a handicap. He did not wish to commit bodily harm on the other, beyond defending himself. And Hsu Fu was out for blood.

It seemed unlikely that the other knew from which direction Alex had come. He must have been as surprised as the intruder when he ran into him in the hall, in spite of his instant reaction. Alex got his back against the corridor wall and, holding his breath so as not to give the other inkling of his location, began to slither down in the direction from which he had come.

The Chinese was fumbling around, muttering in rage at being thwarted. It took several moments for him to realize that the thing to do was to open the door again and flood the hall with light.

When he did, Alex dashed for it. He had lost his black handkerchief mask in the fight but now his back was turned to his foe and he doubted that the other could identify him. He sped down the hall, past the various rooms he had explored, and to the glass door by which he had entered. He hurried through and headed across the street and to the dark of the trees and bushes there.

By the time he reached the ruined mansion which faced on the back of the Sierra Nevada he was definitely feeling the effects of his hectic encounter with Hsu Fu. He ached in a half dozen places. He couldn't remember taking some of the blows that he obviously had. He wondered sourly if he had landed anything at all in return. In spite of the fact that he hadn't wanted to disable the old boy, he hadn't been pulling his punches. He had been in the clutch and desperate. It was fantastic. The wizened Oriental moved with the speed and strength of a man of less than forty. No one older than forty years of age could have duplicated the terrible old man, with the possible exception of a professional Karate teacher in the best of trim. And even a pro couldn't have so performed beyond the age of, say, fifty.

It was an effort to ascend the wall to his terrace, in the same manner he had come down. He allowed himself a few groans in the passage but he walked up the space between the tree and the stone wall as he had descended. Never in his climbing days in the Alps had such a short distance taken equal effort.

On the terrace he stood a long moment breathing. And then it came to him that there was a light in his room. He couldn't remember leaving a light. In fact, he had deliberately kept the room dark while he changed his clothes for this nocturnal escapade.

He sucked in air and headed for the French windows.

Inside, Lilith Eden was seated comfortably in one of the room's several easy chairs.

She took him in with her abnormally wide eyes

from head to toe and her perfect eyebrows went up. "Hello," she said. "Where in the hell have you been?" Her eyes had gone to the terrace from which he had just entered.

He looked at her for a long moment. "Up on the roof," he said. "I didn't know you were here. It's, well, beautiful up there. The stars and all."

She obviously agreed to that. But she said, "You look all sweaty."

He headed for the bathroom. "I've been exercising. I'm an exercise buff. That's why I've got such beautiful muscles."

The sides of her mouth turned down at that.

He closed the door behind him and cleaned up. Thank whatever gods there probably weren't that none of the blows of the Chinese had landed on his face. He could feel them all over his body, kicks and flat hand blows, but none of them had disfigured his face.

He returned to the other room and looked at her. It was well worth the effort; the slim figure, the perfect posture, the small beautiful head atop the ballerina's long graceful neck.

"What did you want?" he said.

She looked at him mockingly, the sides of her mouth turning down. "Can't you guess. You're not very romantic."

3.

When Alex Germain awakened in the morning, it was to find Lilith, her head on the adjoining pillow, staring at him thoughtfully. He realized all over again how startlingly beautiful she was in spite of the fact that she took no effort to accentuate that with which nature had gifted her. He couldn't imagine his early impression of her, there on the bench in the Zócalo, when he had thought her plain.

She had been a charming lover. Quiet, sweet, slow. She'd evinced none of the burning passion of Dulcinea. She soothed, even as she satisfied.

She said, her low, even voice sleepy, "Good morning, darling."

He yawned and said, "Good morning." He eyed her. "I'm still not very clear on just how come you're here." That wasn't quite right. He added quickly, "Not that I don't appreciate it."

"I was lonesome," she said softly, as though that explained all. "You have no idea how lonesome. Who was your visitor last night?"

"Visitor? Only you."

"After you fell asleep, I thought I saw someone out on the terrace. Someone in a kind of black night robe. It was too dark to see very well."

Dulcinea again?

He cleared his throat and said, "It must have been your imagination. There's no way of getting onto the terrace except through here. Well, there's a little staircase going up to the roof. You think it might have been a prowler?"

"I suppose not. As you say, probably my imagination. Just some shadows."

They lay there for a long moment taking each other in, probably each remembering the high points of their intercourse the night before. There was the slightest of flushes at her neck.

She said, suddenly, "Alex, take me away from here. Take me away from San Raphael. Anywhere."

He nodded. "All right. When I go, I'll take you with me."

"I want to go right away. Today. I want to get out of this dry, dull, grim old town."

He sighed. "That's what Nuscha said."

She wrinkled the perfect forehead. "Who's Nuscha?"

"Ursula. Ursula Zavala. Are you working as a team, or did you come up with the same tactics independently?"

She was angry. "I don't know what you mean."

"She wanted to leave town with me too. I used to know her in Europe, a long time ago. But it was obvious what would happen. After we'd had a long lost weekend down at some beach, she would have come back here, with me safely away. I suspect that you'd do the same. I think you both belong here. But for some reason want me to leave."

"And I think you're crazy as hell and withdraw the invitation."

They continued to lie there looking at each other. There seemed to be no rancor in her. In fact, her dark eyes seemed to hold approval of him.

He said abruptly, "Lilith, what nationality are you?"

"I'm an American."

"I mean, where did you originally come from? You know, racially?"

She looked at him for a long moment and the side of her mouth turned down in her characteristic, rather sad smile. "I'm a Cro-Magnon."

He didn't get it at first but then laughed. "I

suppose we all are, aren't we? The first true men. Homo sapiens. But where were your people born? I can't place your face. Southern Italian? Andalusian? Cretean?"

"My first memories are from the vicinity of Altamira, in the Basque country."

"Spain, eh. Altamira. Isn't that where the famous cave paintings are?"

"Yes. My clan did most of them."

He hoisted himself to one elbow and looked at her, scowling. "Your clan? You mean your family? I thought those cave dwelling paintings were accepted as genuine."

"I suppose the clan is what you might call an extended family. They are genuine. The paintings, I mean."

He sank back onto his pillow and laughed again. "Oh, I get it, you're sticking to your story. You're a Cro-Magnon."

"That's right."

"Lilith, eh? The first woman in the world. Lilith of Eden."

"Yes. Perhaps the first. I don't know. But, now, certainly the oldest."

"Something like 25,000 years, eh?"

"More, I suppose. We didn't have calendars."

"It's rather unique. How do you figure it happened?"

"Until a few years ago, I couldn't. Then with the fairly recent discoveries in DNA, genetic manipulation and bioengineering and the advent of space travel, it became more clear. I pieced these developments together along with old tribal stories of ours, legends as we'd say today, and came up with what might make some sense."

"I can't wait to hear."

"When the first extra-terrestrials landed, they found Neanderthal man. He'd evidently been around about 75,000 years or so but seemed to be a dead end. So the extra-terrestrial bioengineers went to work and from Neanderthal developed the Cro-Magnon, Homo sapiens, true man, or whatever you wish to call him."

"Why?"

"How would I know? Possibly just for the hell of it."

"And you were the first."

"I must have been one of the first. There were others. Not many, probably."

"It was really the Garden of Eden then. You all interbred. Cain with his sisters and . . ."

"Oh, no. We bred with the Neanderthals. They've had a bad press, you know. From what I've read in current anthropology, they were the first true men, not the brutes and dumb half-apes that they're usually portrayed as. They had language, art, and even religion, a concept of life after death."

Alex laughed again. "You know," he said. "With a good title and a snappy ending, I could sell this. All right. So you lived on . . . and on. What happened to the others?"

"At first, we were just sort of freak members of the tribe. Then, as it split and split again we were separated and went off along our various ways."

"Why did the tribe, this tribe that the extra-terrestrials subjected to gentic manipulation, split?"

"You have to know something about primitive society, based on the clan. By the way, evidently that's one of the things the extra-terrestrials taught our tribe: gentile society. You have, say, a tribe of four hundred, divided into four clans—the Fox, Wolf, Fish and Deer clans. Tribal taboo forbids you to marry within your own clan. If you're a Fox, you've got to marry a Wolf, Fish or Deer, and so forth. It prevents close interbreeding. The straight Neanderthal tribes didn't practice it. They remained completely promiscuous and over a period of time the new Cro-Magnons became dominant, because we did. At any rate, we split over and over again as we grew in numbers. You see, we were hunters and gatherers and as such couldn't become too numerous in any one area. There wouldn't be enough game to go around. So half of each clan would split off the tribe and go their own way, a new tribe of four hundred."

Alex shook his head in admiration. "You've really got this worked over to a tee. So then what happened?"

"The original specimens that the extra-terrestrials had produced became spaced out. Interbred with the Neanderthals, they became—what would you say?—watered down. Some of the attributes we originally had became diffused in the genes banks, or however you'd put it. I'm no biologist."

"I've already suspected that, sweety. But how come you're still alive and the others aren't?"

"Over the years, over the centuries, I suppose they died by accident, one by one. A saber-tooth, a fall over a cliff, a famine. Perhaps killed by an enemy tribesman. So far as I know, I'm the only one left."

"So you lived on."

"Yes," she said lowly. "I lived on. Perhaps I was

unique, among the different experiments. Among other things, I'm sterile. I don't think most of the others were. They spread their genes."

Alex grinned at her. "After 25,000-odd years, you must be a little tired."

She looked at him emptily. "I was tired before they built the first pyramid along the banks of the Nile, before they molded the first adobe bricks for the tower of Babel."

"Haven't you ever considered suicide?"

"A thousand and more times, Alex. But I have the curse of life. All of my instincts demand that I live. I cannot reject them. Time and time again I have made a firm decision to suicide, in some easy manner, such as an overdose of morphine ... at the end of, say, twenty-five years. But then, when that time has expired, all my mind and body says, No, no. I am always healthy, Alex. If I had the excuse of pain and anguish, perhaps yes, but I have not."

"So you began life as a Cro-Magnon cave woman, living with dumb brutes and ..."

"They weren't dumb brutes. If anything, the Cro-Magnons were probably more intelligent than the average modern man. For one thing, the stupid ones died. Nature did them in before they grew old enough to breed and have their genes reproduced in the next generation."

"If they were so smart, why didn't they invent such things as the wheel?"

"Because they had no use for the wheel at that stage. They were a hunting and gathering society, without domesticated animals. Before even a wheelbarrow makes sense, you've got to have something heavy to move around and fairly smooth ground to move it over. What you're confusing is accumulated knowledge and superior intelligence. You can have one without the other. I, for instance, have a great deal of accumulated knowledge, most of it useless, but I suspect that I am not especially intelligent. I've never had an I.Q. test. Possibly I'm afraid to find out the result, but I suspect I have an I.Q. of 90 or so."

"I'd think that after 25,000 odd years you'd have the wisdom of the ages."

"What wisdom of the ages? You sound like a damn Rosicrucian. We've accumulated more knowledge in the past half century than we did since Cro-Magnon times. Recently, man has been doubling his knowledge in less than every eight years. But it works both ways. He's also losing false knowledge at a fabulous pace. An education today has a half life of about the same time. Eight years. You graduate from college with a doctor's degree in physics. Eight years later, half of what you learned has become antiquated. Eight years later, half of the remaining has become old hat and you're on the trash heap as a physicist, unless you've been keeping up with the new developments. I once saw Benjamin Franklin when he was a man in his seventies, ambassador to France. He was considered one of the most wise men of the time. And was. Today, any graduate of high school knows more than Franklin ever did."

He chuckled. "You sound a little bitter."

She said wearily, "Here's an example of my wisdom, acquired down through the centuries. Back during the Middle Ages I studied alchemy for twenty years or so. I was determined to find out why I was living on and on. I thought that if I found the Elixir of Life and passed it to others, I might find companionship. I might be able to lose the centuries long, aching loneliness. So I studied alchemy under the most advanced scholars in Europe. Do you know how much of it I retain today? That is, how much of it is of use now?"

"No."

"None of it. A lot of god-damned spells and incantations. Twenty years shot to hell. But bring it more up to date. Suppose I'd gone to some medical school a hundred years ago. Would you trust me to prescribe an aspirin tablet for you today? Obviously not."

He was being highly amused. "Well, at least I assume that you're as rich as Midas. All you had to do was put out at compound interest an ounce of gold with some banking house in the 14th Century. By now . . ."

"By now, I'd be as unaffluent as I actually am. Put an ounce of gold out at compound interest and come back in a century to collect and, first of all, the banking house probably no longer exists. But if it did, you'd have your work cut out collecting because you wouldn't be able to prove it was yours. But suppose you were able to prove your identity. You'd probably be arrested as a witch and wind up in one of the Inquisition's dungeons. That is, until quite recently. Nowadays there are other handicaps to an emortal getting rich. Suppose, for instance, I had accumulated $100,000 and wanted to invest it in the year 1900. What would I put it into? Railroads? They were the big thing then.

How rich would I be today, if I'd put my money into railroads? But suppose I had enough of the wisdom of the ages, as you called it, to see the coming of the automobile. Scores of auto companies were springing up. I can think of only two that came down to the present, Ford and Oldsmobile. Undoubtedly, I would have invested, instead, in Studebaker, Hudson, or possibly the Stanley Steamer.''

He had to laugh aloud.

She pursued it. "Or suppose I had that $100,000 in the year 1945, right after the war. Playing it carefully, I might invest in the safest thing going, United States Treasury Bonds. They paid four or five percent in those days, didn't they? I'd net $5,000 a year, enough to live on fairly well in those days. What are those bonds worth today? The paper they're printed upon. It seems inflation reared its ugly head.''

Alex said, "With 25,000 years to play with, sooner or later your luck would have to break.''

"Ummm. So suppose in this day and age in the States I accumulated a million dollars. Then came the day I had to change my identity.''

"Come again? Change your identity?''

"Physically, I appear to be about thirty years of age. Very well, when you're thirty you can present yourself as, say, eighteen, by dressing the right way, cutting your hair the right way, and carefully assuming the gawkiness of the late teenager. Then you can slowly age, altering your appearance just slightly each year. Finally, you can present yourself as, say, forty-five, but not much older before people begin to wonder. So you have to pack your things, including your million bucks and move to a new vicinity where you start out all over again as a teenager. Great. How do you explain the million bucks? Where do you tell the new community and eventually the Internal Revenue Service you got it? When they become suspicious and ask for your Social Security Card and later your proof of citizenship such as your birth certificate, what do you tell them?"

"Why not the truth?"

"And wind up in some institution being examined by a flock of beady-eyed doctors and scientists? They'd never let me out. Have you ever heard of Typhoid Mary? When they finally caught her, she spent her remaining years in sanitariums, hospitals, institutions, although she had committed no crime. It doesn't pay to be a freak in this society."

Alex said softly, "Why are you telling me all this, Lilith?"

It was her turn to laugh and it was sadly sour. "Why not?" she said. "Obviously, you don't believe me. I've never met anyone who believes me . . . Well, not all of it."

"To the contrary," he told her. "I believe every word."

"Clown," she said.

She pushed back the single sheet of bedclothes that covered them and swung her long legs out over the side of the bed. She was nude, breathtakingly, even though he was satiated with sex.

She said, "I'll have to go to work, darling." She headed for the chair where she had left her clothes the night before.

"What do you do?"

She sighed. "I'm the secretary of one of the doctors at the clinica."

"Oh, yes. The town hospital. What do they do there?"

She looked at him from the side of her eyes, even as she took up her underclothing. "It's a hospital," she said. "What in the hell do you think they do there?"

"I passed it yesterday. Seems quite large for a town this size. And there doesn't seem to be a surplus of patients."

She said evasively, "Some of the retirees, here in San Raphael, are quite wealthy. They endowed it. The nearest adequate medical facilities, otherwise, are in Guadalajara, or Mexico City. Too far, in case of emergency."

"I see. But what's the need for all that room? Do they carry on experiments, or something?"

"Experiments?" she said, still dressing, gracefully, beautifully, covering the limbs he remembered so well. She was lying and she wasn't very good at it. "Not as far as I know."

He left the subject, as she pulled her sweater over her head.

"You know," he said. "I still say you look like that bust of Nefertiti."

Her head emerged from the sweater and the sad smile was there.

"As a matter of fact," she told him, "I am . . . or was. That's where I learned my big lesson. Never give cause for large numbers of people to remember you."

"Oh, you posed for that supremely beautiful bust in the Berlin museum, eh? But what was this lesson you learned?"

"My husband, Amenhotep the Pharaoh, was a religious reformer. We left Thebes with all its temples and all its priests and built a new city further down the river. And Amenhotep built new temples to his monotheistic god. The old priests were powerless to stop him. He was Pharaoh. He was also crazy as a bedbug. Most religious reformers are. However, he died. And they came in all their wrath and tore the new city down and the new temples. And the new religion was destroyed." She hesitated. "Well, some of its elements were preserved by the Hebrews."

"The lesson you learned?" he prompted.

"Yes. For fifty years the priests sought me. Didn't you ever wonder why the tomb of Nefertiti was never found? What is the term we use these days? I went to ground. For half a century I hid as a peasant in the mud flats of Egypt. The lesson was, never become visible, maintain as low a profile as possible. Never surface. Never become prominent. Never become very wealthy. Live in such places as San Raphael, not New York, Paris, or Hollywood. Be plain. Don't even wear lipstick. If you are to survive, in this world, become as invisible as possible. Blend into the background."

She slid into her huaracha slippers, looked at him and tossed her head in amusement. "See? I'm the biggest liar since Hitler."

He twisted his mouth. "But I believe every word."

She grinned, puckishly. "Clown," she said again. "I think I'll have a quick breakfast down in the dining room. I'll see you later, darling. In the bar, about six?"

"Okay . . . Nefertiti."

For a moment her face was sad. She shook her head. "Lilith, these days. I have had many names in my time. Lilith I took in a bitter moment for a . . . jest. But for now, Lilith it is."

When she was gone, for a long time he looked at the door which she had closed after her.

He shook his head in rejection. "Poor thing," he said. And then, waxing philosophical, "Of all the human emotions possibly loneliness is the saddest."

He took a deep breath and got out of bed. Still talking aloud to himself, he said, "I suppose it's time for a confrontation."

He showered, shaved and dressed himself in his standard travel clothes, khaki pants and sports shirt, rather than in the dark garments of the night before. He walked over to the window and for a moment stared down into the patio of the Sierra Nevada. Should he pick up Nuscha and take her along? But no. That could come later. For the nonce, Gottlieb was the one to face. And, very possibly, it was just as well that no one else of all concerned knew about it.

He went out on the terrace, ascended the iron stairway to the roof and went to the slight parapet that separated the Sierra Nevada from the adjoining house occupied by the Austrian scientist. Buda was not at his sentry post where he stood watch during the night hours.

Buda, the heavy-set war dog who, as Alex had noted, unobtrusively lay at his master's feet watching all, even in a restaurant, and, when Werner Gottlieb arose to leave the room, trotted ahead and looked out the door, up and down, before the scientist left. Although in his time Alex Germain

had owned many dogs he had never possessed a
Vizsla but he had heard of them, some of the
stories fantastic. For instance, that their combat
instincts were such that they kept fighting after
they were dead. He remembered an ex-Wehrmacht
lieutenant telling him about being confronted with
a Vizsla during the debacle of the last weeks of
Hitler when the Nazis were falling back before the
Red Army and abandoning Budapest. The fighting
dog who had been with the partisans had taken at
least a dozen 9mm slugs from the Schmeisser machine pistols of the lieutenant and a fellow officer.
He kept coming and tore out the throat of the
German captain before finally falling and still, to
the very last, his eyes already glassy, the animal
gave his final feeble efforts toward crawling at the
lieutenant, who still stood there pumping high velocity slugs into the brute's body. The lieutenant,
before the war, had been a veterinarian. He swore
that the Vizsla couldn't possibly have been alive,
by conventional medical standards, for the last
minute or two in which he had continued the impossible fight.

Alex looked up and down the roof but nobody
was in sight. He hadn't expected there to be. He
slung a leg over the parapet and dropped the couple of feet to the roof beyond, which was slightly
lower than that of the Sierra Nevada. The little
room up against which Buda had been lying was
obviously the entrance to a stairway leading below.
The door was open, undoubtedly so that the dog
could come and go.

He considered only a moment before entering
and starting down. It was still early and he rather

doubted that the professor's criada was yet on the scene. Mexican maids were not famed for beginning the day early. It went back to the period when the houses were unheated and the citizens stayed in bed until the sun was well up and providing warmth. Nor was it likely that she was a live-in maid. Not with a single male, no matter how aged. It simply wasn't done. She slept at home.

However, in view of the fact that he didn't know whether or not Werner Gottlieb kept a gun in the house and might wing a shot or two at an intruder, he called out, not too very loudly, "Professor? Professor Gottlieb?"

There was no answer and he arrived at the second floor of the building without either seeing or hearing anything or anyone. Possibly the gerontologist was already down in his 19th-century study-*cum*-living room. Alex headed for the next stairway, down the hall a way. There was a door, half ajar, and intuitively for some reason unknown to him, he gave it a shove and peered in. Beyond was a bedroom, as he had expected.

Halfway between the door and the large bed was Buda, stretched out unconscious or dead.

On the bed was Professor Werner Manfred Gottlieb, or, at least, all that remained of him. The bed was literally soaked with blood. The professor, still in his old-fashioned flannel nightgown was sprawled, sickeningly, his head completely severed from his body. His eyes bulged, still depicting terror. His mouth was wide open and it seemed stuffed with small dried onions. But no, not onions. The stench in the air was that of garlic. The severed head was not the only mutilation. Through the trunk of the thin body, immediately below the rib cage, had been driven what looked like a heavy wooden stake of the type utilized to pin down circus or carnival tents.

Alex Germain's eyes bugged in absolute rejection of the scene.

"Mon Dieu!" he ejaculated in horror.

Interlude

The transceiver in the right hand drawer of his desk hummed and for a moment the old man had to orientate himself before realizing what it was. It had been months since he utilized it last.

He brought it forth, propped it up atop the papers on the surface of the desk and activated it. A face faded in upon the tiny screen.

He said, "Henry: I thought the arrangement was never to contact us unless there was emergency. In these days of electronic spying, who can say what new device might not trace our calls and locate us?"

He who had been addressed as Henry said, "It is an emergency, sir. But the device is almost surely safe. Our people in both Interpol and the Israeli Sherut Bitchon Klali, their internal security, vouch for it."

The sad looking, infinitely tired looking old man said, "What is the emergency, Henry?"

"Unfortunately, we do not have details. But from several sources we have found that something is up. The adversaries seem to have at last amalgamated and have come to a decision, a plan of action against the enclave."

"You have no idea what form this action might take?"

"No. We are working frantically upon it but as yet without success. However, we are convinced that you are in dire peril."

"You think we should dissolve the enclave and reorganize elsewhere? It has taken long years to organize our facilities. For the first time we have achieved suitable laboratories."

Henry shook his head in misery. "Sir, we don't know. It must be up to you to decide. However, there is every indication that already some of their elements are either on their way or have already arrived in San Raphael. He, or they, are professionals, utterly ruthless international hit men, to use the Yankee idiom. If strangers appear in town, beware of them, sir. From this end there is nothing we can do to intervene."

The old man gave a short, low laugh without humor. "And do you think that we, here, can do better?"

"Perhaps you should make immediate plans to evacuate. There is always the proposed base in Kenya."

The sad old man shook his head. "It would take years. And, seemingly, we are right on the verge of success. The professor is enthusiastic."

The other shook his head again. "We will keep in touch and immediately report if we come upon more information. Shalom Alekhem."

"Aleichem Sholem."

The face faded from the transceiver screen.

Chapter 4

Control of human aging is something that
is going to happen. Unless we are slothful or
overcome by disaster, it's probably going to
happen within our lifetimes.
—Alex Comfort
No More Dying

1.

Alex Germain looked about the room bleakly.
There was still horror in his eyes. There was nothing untoward that he could see save what was on
the death bed. It was a most average Mexican
bedroom. On the austere side, if anything. The
bedroom of a Professor Werner Gottlieb who had
little room in his scholar's life for frills.

A gleam near his feet caught his eye. Alex bent
and picked up a spent cartridge. He fingered it
and thought possibly it was still warm but that

could be his imagination. His imagination was
running riot just then. It was 7.65mm caliber. More
often a European load than an American, and
automatic, rather than a revolver.

. He muttered, "When the autopsy is performed,
sure as hell the bullet they find will be silver."

He replaced the brass shell in as near to the
exact spot he had found it as he could remember
and then went over to the dog. There was a gash
and a goodly swelling behind the Vizsla's right
ear. He put a hand on the animal's side and detected heartbeat. Buda was out but not dead.

He looked about the room again trying to remember if he had touched anything. No, he hadn't.
Not even the doorknob. He had pushed the door
open without touching the knob. The only thing he
had touched was the spent cartridge and he doubted
the possibility of lifting even a partial fingerprint
from it, due to its size.

He left the room and headed for the stairway to
the roof. He had to cover himself and do it quickly.
He was a stranger in town and, on top of that, had
admitted that he had known Professor Gottlieb in
the past. In short, he was potentially a prime
suspect. He must not allow the local police to
become sufficiently interested in him to subject
him to a thorough questioning. He was in no position to stand up under a complete interrogation.
And surely if it was revealed just who Warren
Goddard really was, a Nobel laureate going under
an assumed name, it wouldn't be a matter of just
the local cops. Ranking inspectors of the National
Police would be on the scene from Mexico City,
not to speak of the world news media.

Alex Germain needed a perfect alibi and needed it quickly.

He looked up and down with care before emerging onto the roof. There was nobody in sight. It was too early in the day for sunbathers from the Sierra Nevada to be stretched out on the rooftop of that establishment, even if there had been other guests than the Beaumonts and him in the hotel.

He hurried his way down to his room and stood there for a moment in thought. Something came to him and he brought forth his suitcase and dug around in it. He came up with a souvenir he had bought several days before. It was a comb inlaid with carved Mexican jade, a pseudo-pre-Columbian piece. A feminine friend in the States had asked him to keep an eye open for such a comb when he had mentioned a trip to Mexico.

He took it up and headed for the door.

Alex entered the dining room to find it empty except for Lilith, Ursula and Fay Morgan, the librarian. They were seated together, Lilith finishing a light breakfast, Ursula and Fay Morgan with nothing but coffee cups before them. The three of them made a picture: the brunette Fay with her perfect British-Welsh complexion, the tall, blond, blue-eyed Teutonic Ursula, the dark complexioned, almost Negroid, Lilith, the self-proclaimed Cro-Magnon.

He came up and, yawning, without invitation took the fourth chair at the table. Ursula and Fay Morgan raised their eyebrows and Lilith frowned slightly but smiled.

He put the comb before her and said, "You forgot something, honey."

Ursula Zavala and the librarian widened their eyes and then turned them to Lilith.

She flushed and said, "It's not mine."

"But it must be."

"Well, it's not." She stood and threw down her napkin. There was hurt in her dark eyes. "My hero," she said nastily and turned and left.

Ursula looked at him and snorted. "You're a little gauche these days, aren't you, Alex?"

He looked after Lilith, as though in surprise. "What's wrong?" He put the comb back into his shirt pocket.

Fay Morgan cleared his throat and said in deprecation, "Remind me never to spend the night with you, Mr. Germain."

He pretended bewilderment. "Good grief," he said. "We're all grown up adults, aren't we? Who cares who spends the night with who?"

Ursula twisted her mouth and made with her little snort again. "It's a small community, Alex. And particularly the Mexicans take a dim view of, uh, off-the-cuff horizontal refreshments."

Fay Morgan, who was obviously amused by the whole scene, came to her feet and said, "I'd better get to work."

Alex stood too and said, "Going to the library? I'll walk along. There's something I wanted to look up." He was doing his utmost to project himself as he usually did, easy-going, nonchalant, nothing of real importance on his mind.

She hesitated for only a brief moment. "All right," she said. "I suppose I won't be compromised being seen with you on the streets in open daylight."

He said, as though being put upon, "What's that supposed to mean?"

"Oh, shut up, Don Juan," Ursula told him. "Lilith's a nice girl. You shouldn't have embarrassed her like that."

He shook his head. "The older I get, the less I understand you broads."

He followed after the librarian, noting all over again her lush figure. Supposedly the town was composed of decrepit old fogies but between Lilith, Nuscha and Fay there was a surprising variety of pulchritude.

Just as they emerged onto Calle Hospicio, they passed Buda, who was walking erratically, his face dazed.

Fay Morgan said, "Hello, Buda."

The dog ignored her and staggered on his way, into the hotel.

Fay frowned. "I think this is the first time I've ever seen him out of eyesight of the Professor."

Alex looked over at her. "I thought that to you he was Warner Goddard."

She was miffed. "Professor Warner Goddard," she said.

"Oh? Professor of what?"

"How would I know?"

As they walked up the street he said, as though making light conversation, "Does everyone in this town go under a pseudonym?"

Her voice was chill. "How do you mean?"

"Oh, never mind." They turned the corner and started down Calle Recreo in the direction of the postoffice. He said, "What was the dog doing out on the street? I wouldn't expect the professor to allow him to roam."

She said, "Buda can open doors. He's learned how to take a doorknob in his mouth and twist it. For that matter, he'll even paw a bolt and throw it, if a door's locked." She took her heavy bottom lip in her mouth as though she was sorry she'd said that.

"He can?" Alex said in disbelief.

"He's the most highly trained dog I've ever seen. I suppose that Professor Goddard has nothing much else to do with his spare time than train Buda." After a moment, she added, "He's a Vizsla, you know. They're smarter even than Poodles or Weimaraners."

"So I discovered. He thanks you if you scratch his ass."

She obviously didn't approve of the use of the off color word but said nothing.

They passed a ruined mansion he had seen the first time he had walked up this street looking for the Sierra Nevada. The doors were still open and the half dozen men who had been playing dominoes were again at the same game, their jelly glasses of tequila, or whatever they were drinking, on the table.

Alex said, "Is this another of the houses Cohen refuses to sell to such potential buyers as the Beaumonts or myself?"

She looked straight ahead and thought about it a minute before answering. "You have a disquieting way of asking questions, Mr. Germain."

"Alex. I don't seem to be the type person people call mister. Perhaps it's this boyish charm of mine."

"I hadn't noticed. I rather pegged you as a prying type. At any rate, I don't know if the building belongs to Señor Cohen or not. The fact is, the records of the ownership of half the real estate in San Raphael are in confusion. It was more or less a ghost town when the first retirees began to come. There's no reason for a town to be here. No industry, no mining, little agriculture in the immediate vicinity. So it had fallen into ruin."

"Then why did they come?" he said bluntly. Inwardly he was agonizing over whether the body had yet been found but he had to cover by continuing this inane conversation.

She took a deep breath and sighed it out again. "Possibly because it was cheap and the climate is good. And older people, in particular, sometimes find a certain charm in the dilapidated former aristocratic mansions and religious buildings."

"I was surprised when the Beaumonts told me it was impossible for them to find a place. And I ran into the same difficulty. There doesn't seem to be property for sale for newcomers. I'd think the turnover of houses would be continuous."

"Why should it be?"

"Because the median age of the foreign colony seems to be 65 or 70. That means that a retired couple here have only ten years before reaching the average life expectancy. When one dies, I'd think his heirs would put his house on the market. So why can't the Beaumonts find anything?"

She had her lip in her teeth again. She said, finally, "Perhaps because they have been found unacceptable. It's a tight community. They drink too much. Talk too loud. They're a bit, uh, pushy. That sort of thing."

"Me too, eh?"

She looked at him from the side of her dark Welsh eyes. "Perhaps."

He said wryly, "The folks in San Raphael get pushed easy."

They reached the end of the street and turned left on Correo and headed for the Zócola.

"Why do you stay, if the town is so dull?" he said.

She didn't like that question either. Finally, "Perhaps because I like the quiet. I'm kind of a . . . loner, I suppose."

They started across the Zócalo which was all but empty, a few of the benches occupied by playing children and a scattering of oldsters patiently waiting for the sun to bring warmth.

Coming up the portico across the street, hurrying, was David Cohen. He evidently didn't see them. For some reason he seemed in high agitation. Alex inwardly winced. Had the body been found?

And then Alex noted something. There were comparatively few Mexicans on the streets but several, as the owner of half San Raphael passed, crossed themselves unobtrusively. But even more eyebrow raising was the fact that two or three, when the old man's back was turned, made with their hooked fingers the sign of horns to ward off the evil eye.

"What the hell's all that?" he said to Fay.

"What's what?" she said, although he knew very well she had seen the same thing he did.

"Isn't Cohen the mayor, or presidente, or whatever you call them in Mexico? Why are the people afraid of him?"

She shrugged it off. "Some of the older ones are illiterate and superstitious."

He scowled his puzzlement at her. "What's that got to do with it?"

"He's a Jew."

"So what?"

She sighed. "There are very few Jews in Mexico. Those there are live mostly in Mexico City or Monterrey, or the other large cities. Here in the back areas they're practically unknown."

"What in the devil's that got to do with warding off the evil eye when he goes by?"

"The way I understand it, particularly in the past, not so much these days, the priests in these smaller communities are almost as illiterate as their parishioners. They used to tell the peons and Indians that Jews had tails and in their religious rites did such things as sacrifice Christian babies. Nonsense come down from the Middle Ages. After the revolution the authorities took a dim view of such teachings and cracked down but here in the backwaters the more ignorant still believe."

"You've got to be kidding."

"No. You'd be surprised. Not too long ago, the archeologists, particularly down in Yucatan, got into a real dither. It seems that every time some small farmer would plow up a Mayan grave filled with pre-Columbian pots and other artifacts, he'd break the priceless ceramics by kicking them in. The priests had told them the pots were the work of the devil and should be destroyed."

He said, "Between you and Lilith, there seems to be a lot of anti-Church sentiment around here."

She said lowly, "Perhaps we've both had a bit of guff from it in our time."

"If the people are afraid of him, how come he's presidente? Why don't they vote him out?"

"That's not the way things work in Mexico. Theoretically, it's a democracy but in actuality there's only one political party that makes any difference. It's been in power since the revolution. It decides who's going to be mayor, governor, and even president of the Republic. The presidente of San Raphael is picked by the party big shots in Celaya, the State capital. Señor Cohen always keeps in good with them. Sizeable donations to party funds, that sort of thing. So they keep returning him to office. They probably wonder why in the world he wants it."

"So he's not in just for this term, eh? He's been presidente for a long time."

She hesitated for a moment before saying, "Yes."

"How long a time?"

"I wouldn't know. For as long as I've been here."

"How long have you been here?"

The Welsh lilt was gone from her voice. "Damn it, Germain. Mind your own business."

He grinned at her. "I'm thinking of moving to town. I want to find out as much about it as I can. Even about the good looking women who live here. You never know."

They'd arrived at the Biblioteca and Fay Morgan fished a large antique looking key from a pocket in her voluminous skirt and opened up. Alex followed her in.

She said, "What was it you wished to look up? Perhaps I can help you."

"Never mind," he told her. "I know where it is. I saw it yesterday, when I was here."

She shrugged and sat down at her desk and he left for one of the rear rooms. In actuality, he had lied to her. He was going to have to search out what he was looking for but he had no intention of letting Fay Morgan know just what it was.

He didn't have much difficulty locating the material. It was in the same section as he'd found the book on Demonology the day before.

The material on vampires was in a volume titled, *March of the Demons*, by Gary Jennings. He read:

"The vampire's name seems to derive from an old word of the Balkan countries—variously vepir, opyr, etc.—meaning simply 'witch'. But, as popularly envisioned, the vampire was a corpse which refused to stay dead, and continued to roam the land. To sustain this unnatural animation, it had to have human blood, which it drew from unsuspecting sleepers. As with the werewolf, there were various theories as to how the vampire got that way—deliberate defiance of death, family curse, and so on. One theory was that suicides and those who died by violence came back as vampires, and that their bite doomed the bitten one to become a vampire, too, when he or she died.

"Vampires were usually thought of as haunting only the Transylvania province of Romania but the belief has existed in many other far places and times. The ancient Babylonians, for instance, feared a vampire called Akhkharu.

"In other respects, the vampire was rather similar to the werewolf. It was most active during the full of the moon, best killed (or rekilled) with a silver bullet, best buried (so that this time it would stay buried) at a crossroads, and often with a stake driven through its heart to help hold it down."

"Nothing about the garlic," Alex muttered.

After he had finished the passage, he stared at the page for a long moment, unseeingly.

"An act of terrorism," he muttered again, under his breath. "Not just murder but murder in such a manner as to impress someone—or perhaps the whole town. Does Mexico have the vampire legend? Probably. Everybody else seems to."

He put the book back and went to the shelf where he had seen the two volumes by Werner Gottlieb the day before. He took one out and thumbed through it. There was a frontispiece, a portrait of the author in the stiff photography of the 19th Century. The face was that of Werner Gottlieb, a bit younger looking than that of the now slain scientist but undeniably his.

"One hell of a family resemblance," he muttered still again before returning the book to its place.

He left, waving goodbye to Fay Morgan and giving her a cheery thanks.

He went up the street in the direction of the market and, once again, had the feeling of eyes upon him. And once again was unable to locate just who it was that was watching him so curiously. There was nothing he could do about it.

He wandered around the open market which, at this time of day, was just beginning to really come alive. There must have been several hundreds of locals in all, locals and peons in from the campo. In spite of the recent industrialization based on the underground seas of oil that had been found a few decades back, two thirds of the Mexican population were still small farmers, grubbing out a miserable existence on tiny plots of arid land which had long since given up their fertility.

He stopped finally before a ragged Indian squatted next to his wares which were spread out upon a filthy serape on the ground. The handicrafts consisted of hoe heads, machetes and knives, all obviously beaten out on some primitive anvil.

While the Indian watched him emptily, even disinterestedly, Alex bent and picked up one of the knives. The blade was approximately eight inches long and by the looks of it had been fashioned out of an old file. It held a good edge and the point was needle sharp. The handle was hand carved from a very hard wood, probably Mesquite. Alex hefted it. A farmer's knife, meant to be utilized for everything from castrating livestock to chopping down small trees and bushes. It amounted to a small machete. He took it by the blade and hefted it again, thoughtfully. It balanced well and he estimated that it would turn over once in about twenty feet, if thrown correctly.

When it came to bargaining, the Indian was stoical and stolid. He seemingly knew exactly what the product of his labors was worth and would settle for nothing less. Alex gave up and paid over the hundred and fifty pesos. A crude leather sheath came with the knife. Alex wrapped his purchase up in an old piece of newspaper supplied gratis and started back for the hotel. He had forgotten

temporarily about the eyes but now he felt them
again. It was on the irritating side but there was
still nothing to be done about it.

Back in the Sierra Nevada, he entered the patio
to find no one about except Bill and Martha Beaumont seated at a table near the entry to the bar.

They looked at him, somewhat indignantly.
"Where in the hell is everybody?" Bill demanded.
"We can't even get a drink."

"Search me," Alex said and continued on his
way.

As he passed the office he peered in. Nuscha
wasn't there nor anyone else. He went into the
hotel proper and looked into the dining room.
Marcelo wasn't there but two of the waiters were
setting up. Alex went on to his room. He suspected
that the body next door had been found and the
hotel thrown off its routine as a result.

He closed the door and propped a heavy chair
against it. Momentarily, he tossed his package to
the bed. He located the heaviest chair in the room,
a Spanish Colonial replica with a heavy wooden
back and took it to the far end of the room and
reversed it against the wall so that its back was
toward him. He returned to the bed and stripped
the newspaper from his purchase and pulled the
knife from the sheath which he tossed back to the
bed cover.

He stood there for a moment, again testing the
weight and balance of the knife. Yes, he decided,
about twenty feet. He took his stance that distance
from the chair, raised the knife shoulder high and
launched it. The tip buried itself in the wood of

the chair back, the handle slightly high from the horizontal.

"About eighteen feet is nearer to it," he said, going to retrieve the blade for another practice try.

When he was satisfied that he had gotten the feel of his weapon, he returned it to its sheath and buried it in his suitcase. For the time, at least, he couldn't risk carrying it around. Somewhere along in here the police would be turning up and it wouldn't do to be found with it on his person. If they located it in his bag, the explanation was an acceptable one. Lots of gringo tourists bought handtooled Mexican knives. They were picturesque handicrafts.

He returned the chair which he had utilized as a target to its place, its now mutilated back to the wall, and stretched out on the bed to wait. All right, he was ready for them. He had spent the night with Lilith, a respected member of the community, and the morning with the town librarian. His alibi was adequate. He'd had no opportunity to murder the elderly Austrian scientist.

2.

But nobody came.

After a time, he arose and went below. This didn't make much sense. It was now mid-day. Surely, by this time Gottlieb's maid had come to work and discovered the tragedy. Either that, or when Buda had shown up, obviously hurt, somebody from the hotel would have gone to investigate. If so, where was all the to be expected excitement?

When he passed the dining room, he spotted Marcelo and one of the waiters, ready for business.

The Beaumonts were gone from the patio when he crossed to enter the bar. There he found Paco, polishing glasses, and Nuscha and David Cohen seated in the room's farthest corner. Buda, a neat bandage behind his ear, was at their feet. They were deep in low voiced conversation.

Alex nodded to them and took a seat on the adjoining sofa, ignoring Cohen's scowl.

Buda came to his feet, slightly wobbly, and came over to him and put his chin on Alex's knee. His red gold hound eyes came up, despair behind them.

Alex suppressed the compassion that he couldn't allow to express itself before the others in his face. It would let them know he was aware of the dog's terrible loss. He rubbed the Vizsla's ears and said softly, "Hi, Boy. Yes, I know how it is. Everybody likes to get petted. I know. I was a dog once."

Ursula snorted softly at that. "Here, Buda," she said.

The dog ignored her and stretched out at Alex's feet. Alex bent down and scratched his back. "He's all right," he told Ursula. "Dogs are suckers for me. It's my nice smell, I suppose."

Paco came up and said, "Cognac?"

Alex said, "I'll have a Nocha Buena beer. The prices Señora Zavala charges for brandy you'd think she was trying to drive customers away."

"Very funny," she said. "Here, Buda."

The dog wagged his tail slightly, to politely acknowledge her, but remained at his place at Alex's feet.

"Where's the professor?" Alex said. "I have gained

the idea that you couldn't separate him from the dog with a crowbar." Inwardly, he held his breath. He was treading on dangerous ground.

Cohen said, a snap in his voice, "Evidently, Goddard has left town rather precipitately."

Alex made his voice unbelieving. "And deserted the dog?" He reached down and patted Buda again. The Vizsla looked up at him soulfully and hung his long red tongue out.

Ursula said, "All we know is that his few belongings are gone. He left a note for the maid, paying her off." She made her voice go bitter and said, "I suspect it was because of you. He hates journalists and now that you have ferreted him out, took off for some new hiding place."

"Yesterday, I promised I wouldn't write anything about him," Alex said, feeling his way. "But I looked forward to talking some more. He had some interesting things to say about ... gerontology."

"What did he say about gerontology?" Cohen said quickly, and then looked as though he wished he could take that question back.

Ursula said, "Evidently, not much. Alex was telling me about it. David, let me introduce you to Alex Germain. He's a journalist I knew some years ago ..."

"Over twenty years ago," Alex put in.

". . . in Vienna," she went on. "He was supposedly covering one of Werner's meetings."

Paco came up with the beer, neatly served in a heavy mug.

"What do you mean, supposedly?" Alex said, taking an initial sip of the very dark brew.

"I have never seen your byline on anything," she told him. "At any rate, David Cohen, this is Alex Germain."

"We've met," Alex said. "I was considering buying a small place in San Raphael. Señor Cohen seems to think his ruins are worth their weight in silver mines."

"Alex Germain, Alex Germain," Cohen said, his face suddenly thoughtful. "The name, ah, rings a bell. Haven't I met you somewhere before—a long time ago?"

Alex finished his beer in one long swallow. "I doubt it," he said. "To quote Lilith Eden, I've never been there."

He came to his feet. Buda did too.

"Here, Buda," Nuscha said. "You come here with me."

The dog ignored her and trotted toward the door.

Alex looked at him and then at the proprietor of the hotel. "He seems to want to come with me."

"I'll take care of him."

Alex said, "Well, you say he's been deserted. If he wants to switch his alliance, shouldn't he have the say? Maybe he doesn't like women." He twisted his mouth. "At least, human women. I wouldn't know his stand on bitches."

She was furious, her blue eyes glinting, but couldn't think of anything to say.

At the door, Buda looked up and down before preceding his new master.

Alex returned to his room. He had to think this out. A lot of things were falling into place, but some of it wasn't. He sat on the edge of the bed and ran a hand back through his hair in frustration.

The dog came up to him and looked at him woefully. There are no eyes like a hound's eyes for expression. A Bloodhound, a Bassett, a Vizsla.

Alex shook his head. "I'm sorry, old boy," he said softly. "I'll do the best I can for you. Your beloved master is dead. And you know it, don't you?"

"Yiss," the dog said. It came from his mouth as sort of a hiss but there was no denying the meaning.

Alex goggled at him for a long moment before blurting, "You can really talk."

Buda shook his head in a very human-like negative.

"Just a few things, eh? But you can understand?"

The dog gave his stubby tail a feeble wag.

Alex continued to stare. He said, "You're very old, aren't you, Buda?"

"Yiss."

"More than fifteen or twenty years?"

"Yiss."

"More than . . . more than a hundred years old?"

The dog looked at him woefully again and shook his head.

"You don't know?"

Buda shook his head.

"You've had other masters before Werner Gottlieb?"

"Yiss."

"Many masters, one after the other, down through the long years?"

The infinite sadness was in the eyes. "Yiss."

"You are very intelligent, aren't you, Buda?"

The animal shook his head.

That set Alex back. "But you're, well, smarter than other dogs?"

"Yiss."

Alex took in a deep breath and sighed it out. He said, and there was emptiness in his voice, "It's been lonesome, hasn't it, old boy?"

After a time, "Yiss."

Alex Germain hesitated for a long moment before saying then, "You know that I am one of you, don't you? Somehow, you instinctively knew from the first time you saw me."

This time, Buda nodded his head at the same time he said, "Yiss," and he wagged his cropped tail again.

The man sighed again. "All right, Boy. From now on it's you and me. Come along. I've got to check something."

Alex went on out to the terrace, the dog following, wagging gently. They ascended the circular stairway to the roof. As usual, there was no one there. He led the way to the parapet, Buda coming along afterward. However, when they reached the stairway leading down into the house, the dog took over the lead.

Alex said softly, "You're afraid somebody might be here?"

"Yiss," Buda hissed.

They went down the stairs and when they reached the hall, the dog went on to the bedroom in which Alex had earlier found him unconscious with his dead master.

There were no signs of a body, no indication whatsoever of what had taken place in the room. The bed was neatly made. He looked down at the floor. Even the brass cartridge case had been removed.

"All right, let's get out of here," he said. "Cohen's mayor and he and the others have a whole hospital, complete with laboratories, probably complete with disposal units for the remains of dissected animals. If he couldn't cover over, nobody could."

They retraced their way to the bedroom, Buda having some trouble on the circular stairs, as he had coming up, but he managed to navigate them.

Alex looked at his watch. "It's time for lunch," he said. "And in getting my alibi together I missed breakfast. Besides, we've got to keep up the front, for at least a time. Now, look here, Boy. From now on, don't ever say another word in public. Don't ever indicate that you're any different from any other dog. If the bastard scientists ever found out what you are and got you into their laboratories, they'd cut you to pieces and then examine under their microscopes every cell in your body."

He dug into his suitcase and came up with his newly acquired knife and sheath. He pulled his sport shirt out and let the tails hang down over his pants top, hiding the knife in his belt.

"There's no reason not to be carrying this now," he said. "I doubt if the police have heard of the killing and if they have, they were probably involved in the cover-up."

Buda preceded him down the steps. He went first, before they emerged into the patio and quickly looked up and down before Alex came through the door.

Alex grinned down at him. "You make a more

efficient bodyguard than a Secret Service agent,"
he told the dog.

Buda have him the double wag.

Only one of the tables in the patio was occupied.
About it were seated Ursula, David Cohen, Hsu Fu
and a newcomer.

The newcomer was about Alex's own age, tall,
handsome in a rather sardonic Latin twist of face,
and was more flashily dressed than was usual in
San Raphael and certainly the Sierra Nevada.

As Alex and the dog approached, he came to his
feet, his eyebrows raised. He made a somewhat
mocking bow. "So, Monsieur, we meet again."

Alex came to an abrupt, surprised halt.

The other looked about the table at Ursula, Cohen and the Chinese. "Is this the man you've been
worrying about? Let me introduce the notorious
Comte de Saint-Germain, late of the Court of Louis
XV of France, late of a good many other places,
too."

Alex blurted, "Cagliostro! But I thought you were
dead. The Inquisition got you in Italy. You were
tried and condemned to death as a heretic. The
sentence was commuted to perpetual imprison-
ment and you died in the fortress prison of San
Leo."

3.

The other laughed, a cynical note there. "Sit
down, Alex—do you still call yourself Alex among
friends? Sit down before you fall down at the over-
whelming pleasure of seeing me again."

Alex sank into a chair. Buda took his place at his feet.

Ursula looked at him in disgust and did with her snort. "Comte de Saint-Germain? Some American you turned out to be."

Cohen said questioningly, "Late of the Court of Louis XV?"

"Indeed yes. It was of our friend here that Voltaire, who also knew him, wrote, 'He is a man who knows everything.' While Frederick the Great said, 'A man whom no one had been able to understand.'"

Alex closed his eyes in pain. "What in the hell are you doing here, Giuseppe?" he said.

"Probably the same thing you are," the other told him. He looked around at the group. "The Comte de Saint-Germain is first mentioned by the famed composer Jean-Philippe Rameau who states in his memoirs that he met the Comte in Venice in 1710 when he had the appearance of a man of fifty. If so, he was born about 1660. In the years 1737-1742 he was the honored guest of the Shah of Persia. In 1745 the Comte lived in Vienna in the home of Prince Ferdinand von Lobkowitz. In 1749 he arrived in Paris and became the favorite of King Louis and Madame de Pompadour. In fact, the king, who had been bored stiff before his arrival, joined with him in a series of chemical experiments including the making of a group of new dyes, turning base metals into gold and causing diamonds to grow in size. Methinks I detect a certain ability at sleight of hand on the part of friend Alex."

Alex grunted but held his peace.

He whom Alex had called Giuseppe went on. "In 1756 General Robert Clive met the Comte in India and in 1762 he stayed in St. Petersburg, where he took part in the coup d'état which put Catherine the Great on the throne of Russia. In 1768 he was in Berlin and in 1770 was the guest of Count Orloff when the Russian navy anchored at Livorno, Italy. In 1780 some of his music for the violin was published in London. However, in 1784 the church register of Eckernforde, Germany, contains the record of his death, which would have made him 124 years old. However, once again, the next year we find him attending a Freemason conference in Wilhelmsbad. And Stephanie-Felicite, the Comtesse de Genlis, mentions seeing him in Vienna in 1821, in her memoirs. And the Comte de Chalons, French ambassador in Venice, talked with him that same year in the Piazza di San Marco. If you'll add it up, our boy had lived for over 160 years by that time. Oh, Alex gets around."

"You knew each other well in those days?" Hsu Fu said softly.

"Indeed we did," Giuseppe told him. "Between us, we introduced the Rosicrucian movement to Germany."

Alex had finally adjusted to the situation. He looked at the other now and said, "Giuseppe, you've got quite a memory for names and dates."

"It's the cross I bear. I have almost total recall. It is no blessing over a period of centuries."

Alex cast his eyes upward. "Let's see how well I can do. Giuseppe Balsamo, more usually called Count Alessandro Cagliostro. Born in Palermo, Sicily from which he fled after committing some rather ingenious crimes. Visited Greece, Egypt, Arabia, Persia, Malta and Rhodes where he studied alchemy under the Greek Althotas and later with the Grand Master of the Maltese Order. With introductions from the Grand Master he swept through the European capitals, selling elixirs of life, love philtres and mixtures for making women beautiful. They caught up with him in Paris and he spent a bit of time in the Bastille. Afterwards he went to London and spent time there in Fleet prison. Leaving England, he travelled to Rome where he was arrested in 1789. The Holy Office convicted him of heresy but the death sentence was commuted to life and he supposedly died in San Leo prison. Giuseppe, how did you get out of that?"

"That was a very cruel rendition of my 18th Century adventures," the other told him, in mock complaint. "How do you think I got out? The holy fathers proved as susceptible to the elixir of life as did anyone else. I promised a couple of them the secret if they would smuggle me to freedom and pretend that I had died in my cell. I suppose that you and I both came to the same conclusion. We had surfaced in what we thought to be the new Age of Enlightenment, that age of Voltaire and Rousseau in France, Newton in England, Franklin and Jefferson in America. We were premature. Our lives were almost as insecure as if we had revealed ourselves a few centuries earlier. So we both, ah, disappeared again."

Ursula took Alex in acidly. "I should have smelled a rat when you told me you covered that symposium in Vienna over twenty years ago. You would have had to have been about fifteen years old."

"Look who's talking. You and your facelifts."

Cohen said, "Then you are one of us?"

"Evidently."

"Why didn't you reveal yourself sooner?"

"I wanted to be sure. I had heard rumors from time to time of this gathering of the abnormally aged but it is somewhat as Giuseppe has said. It wasn't safe to reveal ourselves in the 18th Century and it still isn't. I needn't point out the fate of Werner Gottlieb." He sighed as he said the last. "Oh, yes, I know about it. I was the first to find the mutilated body. I was afraid to report it. My credentials wouldn't stand close inspection."

He bent and gave the dog at his feet a compassionate rub on the head, then looked up at them again. "Just what is the purpose of this colony of . . . of emortals?"

Cohen shook his head. "There is no such thing as emortals. All life dies, sooner or later. One day the sun will grow cold. One day the galaxy will stop. However, life can be prolonged, it would seem, almost indefinitely. What is our purpose? Largely, to discover why we are exceptions. The youngest among us is at least a century and a half old. How old are you, Alex Germain?"

"Giuseppe's figures were almost correct. I was born in 1665 in the small town of Aix-les-Bains, in Savoy of a French peasant family. Obviously, I am not really a Comte."

Hsu said inquisitively, in a small, gentle voice, "Were your parents long lived?"

"Both died in their fifties."

Cohen said, "Your brothers and sisters?"

"I had none."

Hsu Fu said, "Your children. Have you had children?"

"Yes, on several occasions. However, so far as I know, none were abnormally long lived."

Ursula said, "How do you mean, so far as you know?"

He looked at her. "My aging was arrested at the point that I now look, that is, about thirty-five, Nuscha. I note that the same applies to both you and Giuseppe."

"And to Hsu Fu and myself, for that matter," Cohen said. "But we'll get to that later."

Alex frowned at him, however, he went on. "The aging of my children was not arrested at thirty-five. When last I'd see them, they would be in their thirties or forties. By that time, I'd have to remove myself from their vicinity and change my identity since people would begin to look at me suspiciously. How old are the oldest of you here?"

Cohen said, "I am probably the second oldest. Lilith seems, by far, oldest. She has a rather strange theory about her being the result of genetic manipulations on the part of intelligent visitors from some other star system."

"She told me about it. I suppose there'll never be the evidence to prove it one way or the other."

"Lilith talks too much," Ursula snorted. "You were thought to be an outsider."

"Women confide in me, Nuscha," he told her. "I suppose it's my air of innocent boyish charm." He looked back at Cohen. "How do you account for our longevity?"

The other shook his head. "We don't, thus far. As I say, it was one of the reasons for the forming of this enclave. We are experimenting, seeking the reason. We've come up with a half dozen or more theories."

"What are some of them?"

Cohen twisted his delicate features in a grimace. "Some of them are rather far out, as the Americans say. We even have one of our members who thinks she owes her prolongevity to being a succubus. That is, a fantastically exaggerated sex life. My own belief is that she is simply a mutant who is also a nymphomaniac."

"I've run into her," Alex nodded.

Cagliostro grinned at him. "Et tu, Brutus?"

Ursula snorted.

Alex said, "What else?" He added dryly, "Taking Vitamins C and E and living in Ecuador, Georgia and Pakistan?"

Cohen smiled wanly. "Werner told me about his interview with you. He was trying to brush you off, of course. Just as Ursula, here, and Lilith tried to encourage you to leave town because it was supposedly so dull. We don't like, are even afraid of, strangers in our community. But as to your question. The search for extended life is as old as the race, I suppose. Even the Old Testament gives accounts of persons before the Flood who lived for vastly extended periods. Methuselah, for instance, for 969 years. Adam lived 930 and Seth, his son, for 912. Until recently, we considered these accounts myth, but now I'm not so sure that they aren't legend with some foundation of truth. It would seem very likely, in view of the fact that persons such as Lilith and myself are here today, that the phenomenon has appeared before, down through the ages. Why? How?" He shrugged his thin shoulders. "There have been so many theories proposed that you can almost take your pick. Some of the fiction writers have waxed particularly inventive on the subject. Have you read *Methuselah's Children*, by the late science fiction writer, Heinlein?"

"Yes, as a matter of fact, I have."

"Then you know that in it he proposes two manners in which to prolong life. One of them is to remove the so-called old blood in the body and replace it with young blood, or plasma. It has occurred to me that this basic idea might be the root of the vampire legends."

"How was that again?" Cagliostro said.

Cohen looked over at him. "The vampire story is quite universal. They were immortal, undead, nosferatu, so long as they had blood. They took human blood, but are we sure what they did with it? Are we sure that they simply drank it, like the Masai, one of the healthiest of the African tribes? Or did they utilize it as in *Methuselah's Children*? According to legend, some of the most celebrated vampires were alchemists, some prominent citizens. For instance, Vlad Tepes, upon whom the Dracula story is based, was a Walachian voivode, or ruling prince. One of the cruelest men in history, he impaled literally thousands of victims. Had he wanted blood for transfusions, he would have had little difficulty in securing it."

"Blood transfusion in his day?" Giuseppe scoffed.

"There were some excellent Arabian physicians in his area at that time," Hsu Fu demurred.

"For that matter," Cohen said, "we have the

account of the attempted blood transfusion of Pope Innocent VIII, in 1492. He attempted to gain immortality by having the blood of three young men transfused into his veins. But they were evidently not of his blood type. They didn't know, in those days that incompatibilities of blood proteins were responsible for sometimes fatal results in transfusions. He died."

"All right," Alex said. "Succubi and vampires. What else?"

Ursula laughed lemonishly. "There was the Fountain of Youth that Ponce de León searched for in Florida. Waters bubbling up from the depths of the Earth with mysterious ingredients so that if you bathed you became ever youthful."

Cagliostro chuckled. "And remember Huxley's *After Many A Summer Dies the Swan*? The characters enjoyed prolongevity by eating raw carp guts. Huxley pointed out that carp live indefinitely. There are some in the gardens of Versailles that were first placed in their pools during the reign of Louis XIV."

"Yes, of course," Alex said impatiently. "Or how about Ayesha in H. Rider Haggard's *She*? She became immortal by bathing in a flood of eternal flame that came up out of the ground in a cave in a mountain. But let's get down to reality. Shades of Erich von Däniken, Lilith thinks that extraterrestials toyed with the genes of Neanderthal man and came up with Homo sapiens. But in cross breeding with the Neanderthals the Cro-Magnons watered down their stock, as she puts it, so that the prolongevity features were dissipated and so that now only once in many hundreds of thousands of births, even millions, does a new Homo longevus turn up. Her theory would be hard to prove. What else have you come up with that might be more scientifically valid?"

Cohen accepted the question. "Some of us support the belief that most, if not all, of us are the result of a secret organization, or more than one, going far back into antiquity but which disappeared during the Dark Ages. As a comparison, there are two organizations today, the Rosicrucians and the Freemasons, who claim their origins in Ancient Egypt or Babylon. Plato, in his *Republic*. taught that the naturally superior rules the others and that the race should breed for intelligence. There is no reason why a group couldn't have banded together with the idea of deliberately breeding for prolongevity, in Greece, Egypt, Babylon, India or even China. Heinlein, once again, utilizes the idea in his *Methuselah's Children* but he has his Howard families turning out centenarians within a couple of centuries of selective breeding. It wouldn't seem that such a few generations would have much effect on genetics. However, two or three thousand years are another thing."

A Mexican girl wearing a somewhat soiled white apron came from the kitchen and hurried up to Ursula.

"Señora, Concha y Maria se pelearon otra vez. Se estan jalando los cabellos una con otra."

The hotel manager came quickly to her feet. "Damn it," she said. "I'll kill those two fat slobs. I can't let them out of my sight for fifteen minutes, or they'll start fighting, accidentally drop some soap in the soup, or steal the sugar."

"A broad's work is never done," Cagliostro told her, grinning.

"Shut up, you Wop," she told him, making a beeline for the kitchen to break up the battle going on there.

Alex shook his head and turned back to Cohen sceptically. "If there ever was such an organization, where is it now?"

"It probably would have been suppressed after the Christians became the State religion under Constantine. The famed Mysteries of the Greeks and Romans are still largely secret. Some of them, such as that of Dionysius, had hundreds of thousands of followers but we know practically nothing about what they practiced. The thing is, most people don't realize that when the Christians came to power, the Roman games were not ended. They continued for another century until the Emperor Honorius closed the arenas in 404 A.D. The big difference was that instead of the Pagans throwing the Christians to the lions, the Christians threw the Pagans to the lions. Most, if not all, of the ancient Mysteries sects disappeared during the Dark Ages, done in by the new religion."

"Do you have anyone here in the enclave that belonged to such an organization?"

Cohen shook his head. "No. But you see, most of them would have disappeared in the bad years that followed the collapse of Rome. And others would have died in the plagues, in the wars, by accident—or even suicide. For that matter, perhaps they succeeded in prolonging life only a century or two, at least in most cases. In which instance, they would all be dead by now. However, there would be throwbacks to them which would have emerged from time to time. You and Cagliostro, for example, might be examples. Your parents were not long lived, neither were your children, but the prolongevity genes came out in you. Perhaps a great or great-great grandchild of yours might also be born with the correct combination."

Alex thought about it. "How does that explain such cases as you and especially Lilith?"

"It doesn't and that's one of the weakest points of the theory. However, it's always possible such persons as Lilith and myself were among the founders of the secret prolongevity breeding society. Neither of us were, but I mean our equal number. Which brings us to the third of our more serious possibilities."

"Go on."

Cohen pursed his lips. "Perhaps we are Mutants. We humans didn't always live to seventy, eighty, ninety or even above. It is commonly accepted that three million years ago nobody lived beyond fifty. Nobody. As recently as 300,000 years ago, the maximum life span had been extended to about 77. Today, life expectancy for the average person at birth, in the advanced countries, is about 78 and even higher in such countries as Sweden. But maximum life span is considerably higher and a number of ordinary persons reach to over the 100 mark. I am, of course, not counting such freaks as ourselves, here in the enclave. Given these figures, it can be argued that nature is slowly heading toward immortality for the Homo sapiens. The maximum life span has been more than doubled. If so, is it not quite possible that a mutant is occasionally born who is impervious to death, save by accident, execution, or suicide? If so, it would account for myself as well as Lilith, assuming her own theory is invalid."

Alex looked at him. "Just how old are you, Señor Cohen?"

"Believe me, I was wandering long before the legendary curse that Joshua of Nazareth supposedly put upon me," Cohen said wryly.

Alex's eyebrows went up. "Then you are . . . Ahasuerus?"

"That is correct."

"I suspected it. We now come to the question with which I began. Why are you here? What is the purpose of this enclave?"

"Basically, to protect ourselves."

"From what? From whom?"

"I understand, my dear Alex Germain, that for some years you have evinced an interest in gerontology. That you first met Señora Zavala and Gottlieb at one of his symposiums on the subject."

"That's right."

"Why do you think that research in the field has fallen off so greatly since those days? It was all in the air, then. Now, the average layman never hears of prolongevity anymore."

"I've wondered about that myself. Gottlieb said it was because funding of research was cut so largely that it was unable to continue. That government, foundations and universities cut back as a result of the current economic depression and redirected such funds as they did have into such things as military research."

Cohen shook his head. "That is the excuse we

hear. However, it is not the truth, or, at least, not all of it. You see, Alex Germain, we here in this enclave are natural emortals. We possess prolongevity, although we do not know why. The gerontologists and other scientists on the outside, researching in the field, were looking for an artificial method of attaining to prolonging the life span. There is only one reason for them discontinuing their work."

Alex scowled at him. "What is it?"

"They have discovered the secret they sought."

Interlude

He answered the summons of his communicator nervously.

Before he could make any sort of greeting, the impatient, domineering, military face there snapped, "Where in the fucking hell have you been?"

"Sorry, Chief," he said. "I was out on the street when you called. I had to get back to the privacy of my own place."

"Report, damn it. Did the operation come off as planned? Are they going to have to abandon the enclave and split up so that we can eliminate them one by one, inconspicuously?"

He cleared his throat, apologetically. "I'll have to answer that by saying yes and no, General. The professor has been liquidated in the particular manner I told you about. We thought that when he was found a wave of superstitious fear would go through the town which would result in so much attention that the enclave would break up and head out in all directions. But Cohen, or one of the other leaders, came up with an answer. They evidently smuggled the body out of the house and probably to their laboratories where they could dispose of it. Then they cleaned up the house, making it look as though he had simply left town.''

"You damned incompetent," the other snapped, glaring. "You should have seen that the maid or somebody discovered the body first. You didn't leave any evidence that would reveal your complicity?"

"No, Chief, you can be sure of that. His bastard of a dog ripped open the calf of my leg before we could bash his head in. I've got it bandaged up now but nobody could see the bandage under my pants."

"Did the dog see you? If I understand correctly, the animal is of abnormal intelligence."

"We were disguised and masked."

The face in the screen registered disgust. "Damn it, we didn't want a conspicuous wholesale massacre there in one spot, something can always go wrong. But we can't tolerate them any longer. We can't know at what time they might decide to reveal themselves to the public and then the fat would be in the fire. You're simply going to have to take the chance."

"There's almost two hundred of them," he demurred lowly.

"I'm sending you reinforcements. You'll be contacted in the usual manner. You have equipment on hand but we'll send in more and you have more than adequate funds for a successful, ah, getaway. Do you have any questions?"

"Well . . . I suppose not, Chief. But a thing like this will have world wide repercussions. Two hundred people. Suppose even one of them gets away and sounds off. The whole story you want suppressed would hit every headline and every Tri-Di news program on Earth."

"In the first place, see that not even one of them does evade you. And, in the second place, we are not implicated. No one could lay it at our doorstep. If, by more of your incompetence you or any of the others are apprehended, no matter what, keep your silence, mister. You will be released within hours. We have our resources."

"Okay, Chief. When should we pull this off?"

"As soon as your assistance arrives and you can make adequate plans. Their only chance is to go to the public and that is the one thing we cannot tolerate."

Chapter 5

There is no reason to believe that a century and a sixth is man's immutable maximum life span. . . . If we cannot achieve immortality, we may at least achieve a longer life.

Whether, in view of the population explosion, such a consummation is devoutly to be wished . . . is, however, more than a little uncertain.

—Isaac Asimov
The Biological Sciences

1.

Even as Alex Germain stared at him, Cohen said, "It suddenly occurs to me that particularly Hsu Fu and I should not be seen with you. Not even by other members of the enclave."

The others seated about the table looked questioningly at him. Cohen said, "We have reason to

174

believe our adversaries have either infiltrated San Raphael or are on the verge of doing so. You are supposedly not one of us, so you are comparatively free to wander about, like a tourist, and operate as you see fit. It occurs further to me that with the exception of Cagliostro you are about the only one of our number who has a background of adventure and violence."

"How do you mean?" Alex said.

"Most of us, practically all of us, have survived down through the years by being inconspicuous, mild, self-effacing. Those who have surfaced and revealed themselves are no longer with us. Those who sought extraordinary wealth or power largely, though with a few exceptions, such as myself, eventually wound up as victims. You two have, at least during some periods of your centuries, been adventurers but you have managed to survive as others haven't. Now is the time the enclave particularly needs men of action. I suggest that you contact us only secretly and remain, on the surface, a supposed tourist, in town for a few days."

"I've got a lot of questions to ask and the sooner the better," Alex told him.

Hsu Fu said softly, "Why not ask them of Cagliostro? You are both seemingly young men and it would seem natural that you might meet in the bar, or wherever, and strike up a conversation, even become friends. No spy would deem that untoward. You could also continue your flirtation with Lilith, if you will pardon me, since everyone knows that her task is to meet and associate with any strangers that come to town, doing her best to get them to leave."

"I'd already figured that out," Alex said. "All right. I think you're right. Giuseppe, what do you say we go on into the dining room and have lunch? I can probe you there."

"I'll warn Señora Zavala not to inform anyone else that you're one of us," Cohen said. "You'll be our counter-espionage agent, if the adversaries have smuggled a spy into our ranks."

"The term is a mole," Alex told him, coming to his feet. "Possibly you have a mole planted in the enclave."

Hsu Fu reached out a hand with a black handkerchief and Alex's tiny flashlight in it. "I should return these," he said.

Alex took them, saying wryly, "Thanks. I'd like to have another go round with you sometime in a gym." He put the black silk cloth he had used as a mask the night before into a pocket, the flashlight into another.

The Chinese bowed his head slightly. "It would be a pleasure. You are up on some of the more recent techniques. I would value learning them."

As they walked toward the entry to the dining rooms, Buda going ahead, Alex said, "You know, that ancient looking devil took me last night when I was prowling the hospital."

His companion grunted and said, "If you were as old as he is you'd have some surprises up your sleeve too. He was born in China, long before Marco Polo ever got there. Next to Lilith and Cohen, he must be our oldest."

The dog entered the building first and looked into the dining room before stepping aside for the two humans and then following them.

Except for the, as usual, lonely Beaumonts seated at a table for two in one corner, they were the first two luncheon diners. Marcelo met them at the door, menus under his arm.

Cagliostro said, "Marcelo, you don't have the small dining room reserved, do you? We two would like to bat the breeze, unheard. It seems as though we're both dirty story fans and it wouldn't do for others to hear us."

"Certainly, Señor Balsamo," Marcelo bowed and led the way.

The small dining room held but one table, which would accommodate six or eight. They seated themselves and the dog took his place underneath. Marcelo presented them with menus and left after taking their orders for two Tequila Sours.

Alex said, "Marcelo one of the enclave?"

"Yes, the only one working in the hotel save Ursula. When he eventually finds out you're one of us, if he asks you if you were ever a waiter, or bartender, say no, even if you have been."

"Why?"

"Because he'll try to recruit you. Ideally, this center of ours should be manned solely by enclave members, so that we could talk among ourselves openly. As it is, we've got to watch our conversation, even in front of waiters. If we could get a decent bartender from among our numbers, it would help. Then at least we could talk in the bar. That, by the way, is the reason you see so few of the community in here ordinarily. They eat and drink in each other's homes, so that they're free to talk. Here, they've got to watch themselves."

"There were a good many the first night I arrived. To check me out, I suppose."

"That's right. To see if anyone recognized you as either a friend or enemy. Sometimes, a new potential recruit to the colony comes having heard rumors, just as you did, and often one or the other of us recognizes him or her. When you arrived, just by luck, I was out of town, checking out a prospect."

"How do you mean?"

"We're trying to gather together, here in San Raphael, all of us. All who are naturally extra-long-lived. Things are coming to a head with the enemy and we've got to stick together. So when a rumor comes in, from our various sources, that there's a prospect, I've got to check him out. Usually, it's a false alarm. Anticipating your next question, we have some of our number planted in key positions throughout the world. We even have one in the FBI, another in Interpol. Sometimes I locate some poor prolongevity-prone who is bucking the world all on his own, scared to death he'll be discovered and thrown into institutions, laboratories and hospitals to be examined by the double-domes for the rest of eternity, or until he can bring himself to suicide."

Marcelo came in with the drinks and took their orders. Cagliostro suggested steak with the Bearnaise sauce.

"In Mexico?" Alex said doubtfully.

"Our good Frau Ursula serves the best, and possibly only, steak in the Republic. She practically makes it herself. She starts with the usual tough as leather stuff, marinates it in oil and wine and ages it till hell freezes over."

After Marcelo left, Cagliostro said, "Okay. Fire away with the questions."

"I hardly know where to start." Alex sipped his drink. "For beginners, what's with Buda?" Under the table the dog gave his stub of a tail a wag upon hearing his name from the lips of his new master.

"We don't know much. He showed up and approached Gottlieb at the time Hitler was taking over the Reich. He seemingly instinctively knows our kind when he finds us. He was on the thin and scrawny side. Werner needed a dog like an extra hole in the head but Buda persevered and finally the professor caught on. The dog was a freak of nature, like the rest of us. An emortal thrown up out of the ranks of a species that ordinarily lives only ten or fifteen years. Obviously, Gottlieb took him in and they've been together ever since."

"He's smart, isn't he?"

"No, not especially. He's just long lived and has accumulated knowledge, like the rest of us. Most dogs die before they're old enough to have learned much. That's one of man's greatest advantages. His life span. For instance, until the age of about five, a Chimp is smarter than a human. Then the human forges ahead. Children aren't really able to take care of themselves, make their living and so forth, until the age of fifteen or so. A Chimp is senile or dead by about thirty when man is just really hitting his stride. A dog is dead by fifteen. But Buda lived on. From time to time, he picks up a new trick. You'd be surprised."

"I already have been. Look, what's with the Sierra Nevada?"

The other laughed suddenly and took down part

of his drink. "You know, it's amusing the way we've all taken on protective coloring when it comes to language. I was born Italian, you French, Ursula Rumanian . . ."

"I thought she was Austrian."

". . . but all of us have picked up the knack of assimilating the current idiom of the nationality we currently claim."

Alex laughed too. "You're right. When I first came to America, shortly after I went to ground in Europe, I had to learn to speak the way the natives did. Such terms as Odds Bodkins. And each twenty years or so, you have to up-date it or you stick out like a sore thumb. It was rugged during the hippy era."

Cagliostro said, "The Sierra Nevada is the center of the enclave. Ursula is one of our kingpins, and so is Marcelo. We meet here, hang out here, even have a lecture hall. The natives and tourists are squeezed out by high prices and the cold shoulder. We pretend to pay for our drinks and meals, when strangers are around, but in actuality everything is on the house when members of the enclave are involved."

That surprised Alex. "How come?"

His companion grinned. "The enclave is communism to end all communism. Our people, when they show up, come anywhere from dead broke to as rich as Midas, but usually broke. Ahasuerus, that is, Cohen, is already fantastically filthy with the stuff. He was early on when the silver mines of Guanajuato were being discovered. And so is Hsu Fu. You'll never believe this, but he knows where Montezuma's treasure is hidden. He ought to, the sonofagun helped bury it. When he gets a bit short, he goes down and gets himself some little pre-Columbian gold statue, or whatever, and has it auctioned at Christie's. Nothing so spectacular that it'd draw too much attention but several outstanding pieces that bring top prices. Some of the rest of us turn up in town with various loot acquired from such rackets as international banking, or whatever. So, all in all, San Raphael is possibly the richest small community in the world. And obviously, being the close-knit fellowship we are, we don't begrudge it to poorer members who are actually closer to us than if we were immediate family. For instance, Cohen or Hsu Fu turn over a house to anybody who arrives."

One of the waiters came in with their steaks, baked potato and a mixed salad and with a bottle of San Tomas red.

When the waiter had served them and poured and then exited, Alex took a sip of the excellent Mexican tinto wine and said, "By the way, I noticed the other night that practically everybody stuck to such drinks as limeade and, at most, white wine or beer."

"Sure," Cagliostro said. "Make no mistake about it. It's possible to kill ourselves off by being stupid. Given a goodly cirrhosis of the liver and even a so-called emortal will die before too very long. And inhaling tobacco fumes doesn't do you much more good. So most of us are careful about their vices and their diets. Most are on kind of a perpetual health kick. When you've got a greatly expanded life span, you take care of it more carefully."

Alex sliced into his steak, finding it cooked medium rare and exactly to his taste. He wondered glancingly if Nuscha still remembered from his stay in her pension.

He said, "Look, one of the things that's really puzzled me. How come only half a dozen of us look any younger than sixty-five or so. You, me, Nuscha, Lilith, Fay, Marcelo and the pianist in the bar. By the way, is he one of the enclave?"

The other swallowed his bite of potato and took a sip of the wine before saying, "Jack Fast? Yes, except for you, he's the most recent addition. Came wandering in on his own, the same as you did."

"You're sure he's all right?"

Cagliostro smiled. "We became sure when he proved who he was. Don't you get it? Jack equals John equals Johann. And put a 'u' in it and Fast equals Faust. You never ran into him in the past?"

"No, I didn't, though I heard of him. Had a kind of high reputation, didn't he? Even Martin Luther took a crack at Johann Faust in his writings. In actual life, not quite the character so sympathetically painted by Chris Marlowe and Goethe in their plays. The old story about his selling his soul to the devil in return for a prolonged life. The way I heard it, he didn't have any soul to sell."

The other checkled cynically. "I had quite a reputation myself. Not all of it undeserved. Let's face it, at the time I was on the make, in rebellion against the poverty in which I was born. For that matter, your own reputation wasn't exactly spotless. How did you ever grow those king-size diamonds for Madame de Pompadour and Louis XV?"

"I'll never tell," Alex said. "Look, how about everybody here being old timers?"

They were interrupted momentarily by Marcelo coming in with a plate of scraps for Buda. He put them down before the dog who awarded him with a heart-felt wag. Obviously, the dog and maitre d' were old friends.

When the head waiter was gone, Alex said, "Which reminds me. Where does Buda do his business?"

Cagliostro laughed. "That's one of his tricks. Damnedest thing you've ever seen. He's taught himself to use a human toilet. You've never witnessed anything so ludicrous as that dog balanced on the seat of a toilet, his legs hanging every which gawky way. He hates it when you laugh at him. Of course, he should have some exercise too, the chance to stretch his legs. The professor used to take him for walks into the hills but as it is I don't think that'd be a very good idea since what happened to Gottlieb. You shouldn't be off by yourself. Buda's one hell of a fighting dog but somebody with a high velocity rifle and a scope could pick you both off at a distance."

The waiter had left the bottle of wine on the table before them and now Cagliostro poured more for them before saying, "Let's see, you were asking about the seeming age of the enclave members."

"How do you mean, seeming?"

"Just that. It's easier to 'hide' at age sixty-five or seventy than it is at, say, twenty-five or even thirty-five, your and my seeming years. Younger people don't actually 'see' you, because they aren't interested in you. You're old and hence of small interest. Who wants the company of the aged, except, possibly, people of equal age? And you can pretend to be older even easier than you can pretend to be younger. A man in good physical condition can pretend to be twenty years older than he is more easily than a woman of, say, fifty-five can, no matter how many face lifts, pretend to be thirty-five. He uses, by the way, many of the same devices that she does, only reversed in effect. Conservative clothes, cosmetics, such as graying the hair, the way of walking, carrying a cane. He slows down his movements, while she attempts to be vivacious. Cohen wasn't exaggerating when he mentioned that his age and Hsu Fu's had been arrested at about the same time as ours, at a seeming thirty-five. Nude, they'd look about the way we do."

Alex worried it over as he ate. "But sooner or later, Giuseppe, people are going to wonder why you don't kick off. How do the members here handle that?"

"I suppose Cohen's as good an example as any. He's got it down pat. He's been around here since the latter part of the 16th Century. At the seeming age of about forty-five he imports a woman, supposedly his new wife. After six months or so she leaves and he tells everybody she's gone to Europe. She's left him. Then about nine months later, he informs everybody that she's borne him a son. About thirty years later, when he's seemingly an old man, he takes a trip to Europe to see the boy and word comes back that he died there. So, a couple of months later, here comes the boy. Surprise, surprise, he looks the spittin' image of his father as a young man. He has papers to prove his identity and takes over his father's property. And another cycle has been started. By the time he's ready to pull the switch again, everybody who remembered the last time has died."

"I'll be damned," Alex said. "But everybody can't use the same system."

"No, but some variation on it. When a member supposedly gets to be about ninety, he goes up to the States and doesn't return. But shortly an alleged new gringo turns up who looks to be about sixty. He takes a different house, gets different servants and resumes life in San Raphael. For one thing, all gringos look alike to the Mexicans, especially old ones. If anyone says anything about a resemblance, our enclave member simply reveals that he had an older cousin who once lived here, who looked surprisingly like him."

Alex shook his head in marvel. "I suppose being off in the boondocks like this helps. But what if somebody more intelligent than the largely uneducated locals came along and became suspicious?"

"There is nobody of any great amount of intelligence in town. If one turns up, in one way or the other Cohen gets rid of him or her."

"How? It's one thing preventing the Beaumonts from renting or buying a house here, but suppose one of the local kids grows up to be a smarty?"

"Then David usually sends the kid off to school. Say up to the States to a good college. Upon attaining a doctor's degree in engineering, medicine, or whatever, the fellow would be crazy to return to San Raphael. There's no opportunity to utilize the education here. So he either stays in the States or takes up residence in Mexico City, or some other big town where he's in demand."

"How long's the enclave been going on?"

"Actually, almost from the Spanish Conquest. Hsu Fu and Cohen found each other a long time ago. As the decades and then the centuries went by, one by one others would be located and move in. But it's only been of comparatively recent years that the colony has grown to its present extent. Especially since the arrival of Gottlieb, we've gone out of our way to find new, ah, victims of pro-longevity."

"How do you locate these new colonists?"

"It's not as difficult as all that. Most of us know one or two others, sometimes relatives. In the same manner as you and I knew each other during the 18th Century. So a newcomer, once ensconced in San Raphael, sends out feelers to locate the others he knows to be long lived. Most of them are anxious to move in as well. It's too much of a burden to be a freak who has to hide his true age on the outside. Here we can be open and free among each other."

"How about the hospital?"

"You said you were prowling it last night. You must have seen. Actually, of course, it's a real hospital but it's also a front for our laboratories. Down through the ages, we've tried to figure out just what made us tick, why prolongevity applied to us but not to the race as a whole. If we could find out why, then, I suppose, we could achieve real emortality for us all, as Lilith and Cohen seem to have it as individuals. As it is, some of us here in the enclave will live to be a hundred and fifty or so, no more. Some of us live for a couple of centuries and then die. Some, such as ourselves, for at least several centuries. When Gottlieb came, one of the top gerontologist scientists, we really got under way and he thought he was on the verge of finding the real cause of senescence. But his murder will be one hell of a setback."

A waiter came in and cleared off the table but when he was through the two stayed on, dawdling over their coffee.

Alex said, "Well, I suppose we now get to the nitty-gritty. Cohen mentioned our adversaries, the enemy. Who are they?"

"Why, he told you. The gerontologists and biochemists. They've finally made their breakthrough. Which one of the various paths that were being taken, we don't know. The inhibition of the free radicals by oxidating agents, or the immunosuppression, inhibiting the destruction activities of antibodies, or possibly they located the so called 'death clock' that turns off the genes one by one after a certain age is reached. Or possibly they came up with something absolutely new."

"Are you out of your mind, Giuseppe? The enemy? They're scientists!"

The other twisted his face cynically. "Yeah and their strength like Galahad's, is the strength of ten because their hearts are pure. And why are their hearts pure? Because they've spent a few years studying and working in their respective sciences. Come off it, Alex. Being a scientist doesn't beatify you. The boys who presented us with the atomic bomb didn't withhold it. They didn't even put up a beef when Truman decided to drop it on Jap cities. And afterwards, did they resign in protest? Hell no, they continued to work, most, though not all of them, on bigger and better nuclear bombs. For decades something like half the research scientists in the country were working for the military. Did they protest and quit? No. The jobs were well paying and offered prestige. The fact of the matter is, most scientists are like everyone else, out for Number One."

"What do you think happened?"

"We're not sure but we think that one team, or group, of gerontologists and biologists, or whoever else might have been involved, hit upon the answer to creating prolongevity. They kept it to themselves and utilizing care went first, probably, to elements in the power elite, in short they went to big money. In turn the power elite brought elements of the government and the military into it. All of them together must be a comparative handful. But they had the ability to turn off further research. They simply cut off both governmental and private funding of further research and downplayed the field in the news media."

Alex grimaced at him. "But why? Why not just announce the discovery and make it available?"

"You ought to be able to figure that out, man. It would mean the end of the world as we know it. It certainly would mean the end of our present socio-economic system."

Alex said, "Nuscha brought up Social Security, veterans' pensions, and all other pensions for that matter. But there should be some way of solving that."

"That's just one thing. How about the population explosion? I know, I know. It's become a thing of the past in Western Europe and North America. Some of the European countries have actually been losing population since as far back as 1976 and in the United States we have a zero growth rate. It's almost as though nature foresaw the coming of prolongevity and introduced a declining birth rate. But it still doesn't apply to such countries as India, nor to most of Africa and Latin America. Would you try to keep the secret from India? Once it was released elsewhere, you couldn't. What would happen when the population of India lived on indefinitely, rather than dying, as at present, after a life expectancy of about 35? Lived on and continued to breed uncontrollably."

"We'd have to introduce a crash birth control program."

Cagliostro laughed bitterly. "We sure as hell would but you'd have to have world government to make it effective. And would either the free enterprise of the West or the Statism of the Soviet Complex survive a world government? But that's probably not the big worry of our scientist friends, though it would be for the power elite, the politician bigwigs and the military. The scientists are probably worrying about the possible stagnation of the human species and the end of its evolution."

"Oh, come on now."

"Figure it through, Alex. Emortality would mean that eventually the population would grow so large that we could have no more children. Only enough to replace those who died through accident and suicide. And with no new generations of children there would be no more evolution. Period. Stagnation. And the species that stagnates eventually dies. I can off-hand think of one exception, the cockroach. They have evidently continued unchanging for millions of years, but who wants to be the equivalent of the cockroach?"

The other was staring at him, an element of frustration there.

Cagliostro rubbed his chin and said, "Have you ever read anything speculating on the presence of super-intelligent life on other worlds, in other star systems? The question is finally asked, if there are such super-intelligences, why haven't they contacted us? And one answer is that they don't exist. When they had advanced to the point where they achieved emortality, they stopped evolving and stagnated. Just as we would."

Alex said, "For Christ sakes, Giuseppe, you sound as though you agree with our adversaries. Why don't you join up with them?"

"Because they don't want me. And they don't want you, either. They want us both, and this enclave, out of the way. We're a potential danger to them. We're naturally prolongevity-prone. And if the word got out that we existed, a world-wide howl would go up that would force gerontology research to resume at a rate far beyond the former investigations. And sooner or later the secret would out that our scientists had already discovered the secret of extending life. No, they want to get rid of us, Alex, and I, for one, am too used to living to stop at this point."

2.

Alex said, "I still can't believe a group of biologists and gerontologists could have ordered or even condoned that brutal murder of Werner Gottlieb."

"They didn't have to," his old time friend said

patiently. "That isn't the way it works in the cold-blooded modern world, Alex. You're on the wide-eyed innocent side. Look, suppose there's a multi-national corporation that produces soap. They depend on millions of tons of copra a year for their coconut oil. One of their biggest sources is a backward African nation where the poverty-stricken natives will work for a couple of dollars a day. Okay, there's a revolution in the country and the guy who comes to power promises to triple the pay of the coconut pickers. It would make the cost of copra prohibitive so the multi-national goes into action. Their department of dirty tricks moves in. The new leader is branded a leftist. His enemies are supplied with plenty of money and guns. That doesn't work so some attempts are made on his life, not necessarily by the multi-national boys, necessarily. There are always malcontents ready to take a shot at a chief of state, if you'll supply them with the necessary equipment and know how. If worse comes to worst, you can always send in the CIA to make doubly sure the Soviets aren't behind the new Chief of State."

"Getting kind of far out, aren't you?"

"Hell no. The so-called banana republics in Central America were dominated by American fruit companies for a century. Dictatorships were supported to be sure no unions demanding higher pay for the banana pickers were formed. Often, the American marines were sent in to maintain the dictators in power. But the point I'm making is this. The president of the multi-national soap company doesn't dirty his hands directly with all this cloak and dagger stuff. He's a very nice guy, personally. So is the whole board of directors of the company. The dirty work is done by highly paid professionals. And often the things they do aren't even known about by the company's president and the board. And that's probably the way it is with our scientists."

"All right," Alex said, suddenly tired of the long talk. "What do we do now, Giuseppe?"

"By the looks of it, we two are the armed forces of the enclave. Until Cohen, Hsu Fu and the rest decide what to do, we'll have to run interference."

"Aren't there any others we can call on?"

"No, Cohen was right. All the rest of them are meek and mild. They've survived by being inconspicuous, subservient. Those that weren't, died being burnt as witches, or whatever. Except for us, Ursula's the best man in the enclave when it comes down to toughness."

"How about Jack Fast?"

"If I read him correctly, he's not to be trusted in the clutch. I had a run-in with him once. He backed down. I suspect he's yellow. By the way, are you heeled?"

"No. I didn't want to take the chance, crossing the border. Besides, I had no idea I'd be needing a shooter."

"I know you can handle them. I remember some of the duels you had in the old days. Well, happily, I've got a supply of, uh, munitions."

Alex was surprised. "Where'd it come from?"

"Cohen. Given money, you can buy anything in Mexico. With his connections we could get an anti-aircraft gun to mount on the roof. If it wasn't too conspicuous, we might at that. The whole idea of this enclave is to stay inconspicuous. I've got the arsenal at my house a ways down the street. However, I don't think it's a good idea to overdo you and me being seen together. I'll come back tonight at about twelve and pick you up and we'll go and get you outfitted."

He stood. "I'll go out first. Let's not overdo this buddy-buddy stuff. Whoever our spy is, might become suspicious."

After he was gone, Alex remained for a few minutes. His coffee was long since cold and he had half a mind to call the waiter and get a cognac. But no, the wine had been enough. He couldn't afford a less than clear head. Too many curves were being thrown at him.

When he left, he was surprised to see Bill and Martha Beaumont still seated at their table. They had drinks before them and looked completely bored. He wondered why they stayed on in a town when so obviously it had rejected their enthusiasm. He felt a little embarrassed at having largely avoided their advances himself. They had indicated several times that they would have enjoyed his company.

He said, as he began to pass, "You two don't look particularly happy today."

Bill grunted disgust at that and pushed his glasses back further on the bridge of his nose with a forefinger. He said, "I'm beginning to think that Lilith girl is right. This is the deadest town in Mexico."

The dowdy Martha said, her voice with a whining quality, "I'm about of a mind to leave and go on down to Cuernavaca."

Alex said sympathetically, "There certainly isn't much action here. I don't know if I'll be staying much longer either. In fact, I'm beginning to wonder why I'm here at all."

A somewhat strange look came to Martha Beaumont's eyes and she said, "It's a long life."

Which seemed out of context but Alex said, "It sure is," before going on, the dog, as always, leading the way, his golden red eyes alert.

They mounted the stairs to the room and immediately outside the door the dog stopped and growled very softly.

Alex looked at him. "Somebody in there, Buda?" he said in a whisper.

"Yiss." The Vizsla shifted his heavy shoulders in an almost human manner, as though preparing for action.

"There's not much we can do except see who. Let's go."

He flung open the door.

Lilith sat patiently in one of the room's more comfortable chairs, her long hands in her lap, her ballerina posture insisting on bringing to mind her aristocratic projection in spite of her informality of clothing and hair-do.

Alex said, "Hello. Sorry. If I'd known you were here I would have come sooner."

She said, "I puzzled out the reason for that scene this morning before Ursula and Fay."

"Oh?" he said warily.

"Yes. You must have needed an alibi, indication that you were with me at the time of Werner's murder. Did you kill him, Alex? Perhaps you could have done it either before or after I slept with you.

You looked somewhat strange when you came in last night and found me here."

Obviously, there was nothing for it now but to let her in on the situation. He pulled up a chair and sat on it, taking her hands in his own.

"No," he said. "I didn't. However, I must have been the first to discover his body. I went to his house to confront him this morning after you left, and found him."

Buda came over and put his head in her lap and looked up at her soulfully. On the face of it, they were old friends.

"Hi, old man," she said softly. "I'm so sorry for you." She disengaged one of her hands from Alex's and pulled one of the dog's ears gently. "You seem to have adopted Alex. I doubt if you would have had he been guilty."

The animal stirred his stubby tail.

Alex said, "Lilith, I'm one of you. I've already gotten together with Ahasuerus, Hsu Fu, Cagliostro and Nuscha. For the present, we're keeping secret the fact that I'm a new recruit to the enclave."

She wrinkled her smooth forehead. "But why?"

"Obviously, someone is trying to destroy this community. The manner of Werner's death was such that the killer must have been trying to create a furor of such magnitude that the whole country's attention would be turned on San Raphael and the enclave, in the spotlight, would have to disband. At least, that's one way of explaining it."

"But what's this got to do with you?"

He said dryly, "It would seem that Cagliostro and I are the only two men of action that the community boasts. As it is, only the four of you, now five, know I'm one of your number. Cohen thinks I'll be in a better position to ferret out the traitor, if it remains a secret."

She nodded to that and unconsciously ran her hand over the dog's long hound's ears again, in thought. Buda hung his tongue out and panted in pleasure.

Alex said, "As a newcomer, I'm not up on all the angles but it would seem to me that it might be a better idea if we did disband. As it is, we're sitting ducks. The enemy now knows where we are. They can come and get us whenever they want."

She said, "Possibly, but, as you say, there are angles. We have a certain strength all here together. You're an example of how a stranger stands out when he comes to town. So are that Texas couple. And David Cohen and Hsu Fu control this pueblo, including the police. If an enemy were to show up he'd immediately be spotted. And Cohen not only has clout in San Raphael but with the politicians in the State capital as well. He's in a position to run anyone out of town that he wished. Mexican authorities can be very arbitrary if they want. Most likely, any potential enemy would come in with tourist papers, as you probably did, a tourist pass good for six months. Cohen could have his police pick up a stranger on just about any excuse at all. Such as being drunk and disorderly, or insulting a Mexican girl on the street. He wouldn't need proof. There'd be no one to refute the charge. They'd take him to Celaya, under armed guard, and take the train there escorting him to the border. No one would begin to doubt Cohen's story that the fellow was an undesirable tourist. If David dropped the word, which is unlikely since he is actually a great gentleman, the man might be beaten up a bit, just to encourage him not to return."

"All right," Alex said. "I suppose that it's up to whatever kind of enclave government you've developed. I'm too newly on the scene to have any valid opinions. Sorry about this morning, but as you said, at that time I thought I needed an alibi immediately."

"That's all right, darling." She stood. "I'd better get back to the square. The bus is due in and my job is to meet all buses and contact any newcomers."

He smiled at her. "And tell them what a lousy place San Raphael is."

"That's right."

He stood too and took up her two hands again and looked into her face. "What's our status, sweety?"

Her mouth quirked a bit in her quiet amusement but far back in her dark eyes there was a deep pit of loneliness. She said, "About once every century or so I fall in love . . . darling."

He smiled again. "By coincidence, the same thing happens to me."

He took her into his arms and kissed her gently. "Later," he said.

"Of course. And now I'll have to hurry."

When she was gone, he stretched out on the bed, put his hands under his head and stared up at the vigas in the ceiling. Damn it, he didn't like inactivity. Things were developing too rapidly for him to be laying around waiting for midnight and his date with Cagliostro to arm himself. Whoever the enemy amidst them might be, he was undoubtedly currently up to something. His brutal murder of Gottlieb couldn't have had the results he had hoped for. Cohen had covered it. So now the foe must be up to new plans. And what might they be? He or they, come to think of it. There would well be more than one.

Alex Germain wasn't happy at the position he had gotten himself into. It was all very well Ahasuerus—that is, Cohen—saying that Alex and Cagliostro were the only men in the enclave with backgrounds in violence. Although, come to think of it, Hsu Fu wasn't exactly a milk-sop when the chips were down. However, the Chinese probably had the spirit but not the way, limited to his Kenpo and Nanpa Ken and knowing nothing about weapons. And hand to hand combat is fine but doesn't avail you much when your foe is twenty or thirty feet off and has a gun.

The thing was, Alex wasn't up on modern violence much more than anyone else in the enclave. He had put that behind him after he had gone into hiding again following his period of activities during the 18th Century. He was very well aware of the adage that he who lives by the sword dies by the sword and like his old acquaintance Cagliostro he had become too used to living to want to stop. For a century and a half, now, he had kept a low image. Yes, he had taken some courses in various supposed sports, while he had lived for a time in New York. Such "sports" as Karate, commando style knife fighting and small arms target practice. It was amazing what you could study in New York, given the funds. But he had refrained from ever getting himself into positions where he had needed to utilize his new arts. They were insurance, not preparation for adventure, as Cohen had called it.

When he had started this trip, it had been more of a matter of curiosity than anything else. For years he had heard vague rumors of a settlement of the long-lived. He had merely come to check it out, not expecting to reveal himself. And now, here he was, the community's strong arm man.

All his inclinations were to clear out. Wasn't Gottlieb's fate enough of a warning? Clear out with Lilith and the dog, return to the States and go into hiding again. He had a half dozen professions he could make a living at. For that matter, he had a nest egg, an emergency fund, that would keep them going for years if necessary. And he suspected that Lilith would have the same. So, probably, did just about any of the emortals. Over the centuries, too often unknowns would develop which demanded that one abandon his luggage, his accumulated property, and disappear to assume a new identity some place far away and among strangers.

Yes, that was his inclination. But what about Nuscha, Cohen, Hsu Fu and Cagliostro, besides Lilith? These were his people. For more than three centuries now, he hadn't had real people of his own. Temporary friends, yes, even wives and children. But they had all been so temporary. A few decades at most and then they were gone. With all the pain and misery that meant. It was something like having a pet. You grew to love it and then, after a few years, it was gone. Long ago, Alex Germain had given up owning dogs, which he by nature loved. It was too wrenching when they died. And even longer ago he had given up family life. How can you watch beloved wives, daughters and sons wither away with age?

Thinking of dogs reminded him of Buda and he looked down to where the Vizsla was stretched out on the colorful Mexican rug. The animal was asleep, his chin on his crossed paws, breathing deeply. His skin twitched and his legs jerked in his sleep and Alex suspected that he dreamed of the tragedy suffered by his decades-long master. The dog had seemingly largely recovered from the blow to the head he had taken. It was probably that he had greater than ordinary recuperative powers.

The effect of the altitude was still upon Alex Germain and inadvertently he fell off into a nap.

He was awakened by a low growl from Buda. He came instantly fully awake and alert and arose to one elbow. The dog was facing the doorway. However, the door opened to reveal Lilith again and she entered, her face in frown. Alex got up to greet her.

But before he could speak, she said, "Damn it, Alex, there are two men in town."

He sat down on the edge of the bed again, and looked at her. "Came in on the bus?"

"No. They were in one of those Volks mini-hover-caravans. They came from the direction of Quere-tero and the license plate indicated it was a rental from Mexico City. They stopped in the square to ask directions and since their Spanish was rather poor, I had the excuse to come over and ask if I could help them. They were obviously Americans. Very tough looking, competent looking Americans."

"What did they want?"

"A hotel. I suggested that they ought to continue on to Celaya where there were some good hotels and restaurants but they weren't having any. So then I suggested that they come here to the Sierra Nevada, so that everybody could take a look at them—the same as I did when you turned up. But for no good reason at all, they asked about another place. I finally suggested the Villa Jacarama over at Aldama 53, a little dump of a pad for Mexican commercial travelers."

"A flea bag with no private baths?"

She was obviously worried. "That's right. David and Hsu Fu have discouraged any even moderately decent hotels from being built, to keep out tourists and other travelers or vacationists. They won't sell land or potentially renovatable buildings to would-be hotel builders. But they've got to allow two or three third rate hotels for second class businessmen, salesmen and so forth, and the Jacarama is one of them."

Alex stood and paced for a moment while she sank into a chair.

He said, "You notice anything else?"

"They had quite a bit of luggage in the back. Big heavy suitcases and a guitar case and two golf bags."

"A guitar case! Back in Al Capone's day there used to be a gag about the hit men carrying around their tommyguns in violin cases. In a guitar case you could carry one of those small Russian bazookas. Were the tops of the golf bags covered?"

She thought back. "Yes."

"An ideal way of carrying assault rifles. Damn it. Have you told anybody else?"

"Ursula. She's going to get in touch with Cohen."

"Can he have them run out of town?"

"They haven't done anything yet. He's got to have some excuse. They have to be in a bar, or something, where the police can pick them up as drunks or whatever. Alex, possibly they're perfectly okay. Just passing through."

"How much traffic do you get from Mexico City just passing through?"

"Practically none. The road San Raphael is on is out of the way and in poor shape. Cohen sees that this area never gets road appropriations."

"And nobody with enough money to rent a Volks mini-caravan and who's carrying golf clubs and expensive luggage would ever go to a flea bag of a hotel such as the Jacarama."

She looked miserable and afraid.

He said, "Come on. Let's go down to the bar. We'll sit at a table outside in the patio. I should be there in case they show up. If they do, maybe we can call in the police on a charge that one of them attempted to molest Mrs. Beaumont."

"Oh, it's not funny, Alex."

"I didn't think it was. Come on, Buda."

They took a table and Paco came out and received their orders, cognac for Alex, white wine for Lilith. Buda took his place half under the table, his eyes on the Sierra Nevada's entry. Inside, they could hear Jack Fast tinkling on his piano. He was playing "Alexander's Ragtime Band."

After the drinks were delivered and the bartender

returned to his post, Alex said, "You haven't seen Cagliostro, have you?"

"No."

"Can you get in touch with him?"

"He doesn't have a phone. He doesn't like them. Says they're always ringing."

"That sounds like him, the flaky bastard."

He took down half his brandy in a gulp, realizing it was a criminal act with stone age cognac. "Damn it," he said. "I wish I had one of the guns Giuseppe promised me."

"You don't think . . . you don't think it might come to shooting?"

He was irritated with her. "You didn't see Werner's body."

Marcelo came out of the office and approached and said to Lilith, "Señor Cohen would like to speak with you."

She came to her feet, saying, "He's on the phone?"

"He wished you to come to his house, Señorita Eden."

She looked at Alex.

He said, "He probably wants to ask you about the two."

Marcelo took him in a bit questioningly but turned and headed for the dining room.

"All right," she said. "I'll be back as soon as I can, darling."

Only moments after she had gone, from the side of his eyes he could see the Beaumonts emerging from the hotel and starting in the direction of the bar. He was in no mood to sit and drink with them, so he got up and, taking his glass with him, entered the bar proper. Thinking that if he sat alone, they might join him, forcing their company, he went down to the end of the room and sat at a small table, nearest the pianist.

Jack Fast grinned at him in his artificial hail-fellow-well-met mannerism and said, "Any special request, friend?"

"Yeah," Alex said glumly. "The Internationale."

Fast chuckled. "I'm afraid you've got me there. It's an old timer, true enough, but it's the wrong country for me."

A flash of the intuition which he didn't understand but which on rare occasion came to him, hit and Alex said carefully, "It's a long life."

Fast shot a quick glance at him. "If the road is known," he hissed so softly as hardly to be heard, although there was only one other occupant of the bar and he one of the enclave elders at the other end of the room, perusing a magazine, a limeade before him.

Alex didn't know where to go from there and made a show of swirling the cognac in the snifter glass and sampling the bouquet before sipping.

Fast said softly, "Who sent you, the Chief?"

"Of course," Alex said, feeling his way along. "I would have contacted you sooner but I didn't make you." He made his voice go admiring. "You've got yourself good cover here."

The other wasn't above flattery. He all but smirked as he said, "I worked at it. Took time. But now I'm really in with them."

Alex said, "Just a minute. I'll be back. I've got to check something."

He stood and said, "Come on Buda."

The dog had been standing there, looking at

Jack Fast strangely, as though there was a question. He hesitated only momentarily and then turned and trotted toward the door, as usual to check out the situation before his new master emerged.

Bill and Martha Beaumont were seated at what was evidently their favorite patio table and Paco had already brought them Margaritas.

Alex came up and took one of the chairs and said, "Could I join you?"

"Heck, yes," Bill told him. "We three seem to be the only real folks in this here town. Have a drink."

Alex wiggled the glass he held. "Already got this one. Thanks." He turned and looked at Martha and said, his voice low, "Earlier today, when we were in the dining room, I had my head all tied up with other things. It didn't come to me what you said until later. You said, 'It's a long life.' I should have answered, 'If the road is known.' "

They both looked at him emptily and suddenly they were no longer small town Texans.

Martha said, "Why didn't you?" There was no touch of southeastern Texas in her voice, which was harsh.

He snorted self deprecation. "Because in a million years I wouldn't have thought you were working under the Chief." He tried to repeat the flattery he'd given Fast. "Those clothes and all."

Martha's eyes weren't as warm as all that. She said, "Somerlott said he was sending in others but he didn't say who."

Alex nodded, his mind racing. "Two more of the boys showed up this afternoon. They're staying at the Jacarama. They seem to have brought some hardware."

Bill said, steel in his eyes behind the glasses, but relaxing a little, "Who are they, Nick and Dino?"

"I don't know them. If you ask me, this whole operation is a confused mess. I've never operated even with you two before. If you ask me, Somerlott's moving too fast."

"Nobody asked you," Martha said. She seemed some ten years younger and now hard, rather than dumpy.

"No, of course not. I'm just a hired hand." Alex came to his feet. "I've got to do something. I'll get in touch with you soonest."

He turned and reentered the bar and returned to his table next to Jack Fast.

He said, "You probably know a couple more of the operatives pulled in an hour ago. It's probably Nick and Gino. I suppose Somerlott told you they were coming."

Jack Fast eyed him, some suspicion there in the background. "I know Nick and Gino. We've worked together, off and on, since this whole thing broke. Somerlott said he was sending in some muscle but he didn't say who. Who in the hell are you?"

"I've been operating in the Orient," Alex told him, off the top of his head. "We wouldn't have run into each other."

The pianist, who was rippling off, "I Wonder What Became of Sally, That Old Gal of Mine," said, "The Orient! What the hell are you talking about, friend?"

"You'll never believe it, but there was another enclave over in China. And I say advisedly, was."

"Oh." The piano player looked at him with new respect. "Okay, that's something I don't know about." He looked unhappily at the customer at the other end of the room, even though that worthy couldn't possibly be hearing their low voiced conversation.

"Look," Alex said. "How about coming up to my room so we can talk? I got briefed in a matter of no time flat. You'll have to fill me in."

The other nodded to that. "I'll come in over the roof, down to your terrace so nobody will see me. Be there in fifteen minutes."

3.

Jack Fast turned up in even less than the fifteen minutes. Alex was waiting for him, a half bottle of Martell cognac sitting on the room's center table along with two glasses. The dog came to his feet and growled lowly when the other entered through the French windows leading onto the terrace.

Alex said, "That's all, Buda."

Jack Fast was less than the bright smiling pianist he usually projected. He had an aggressive air. He picked up the bottle of brandy Alex had gotten from Marcelo and poured himself a short drink.

He said, "Just to get things straight here, I'm the senior man on this job. Got it, friend?"

"That's all right with me," Alex said. "You've been on the scene. You know the drill. Like I said, I've hardly been briefed at all. I suppose the Chief left it for you."

"Okay. Any immediate questions?" Fast took a chair.

Alex poured for himself, then settled down in his

own seat. "Frankly, I'll tell you the truth, this is the damnedest assignment I've ever been on. This and the China deal."

"It sure as hell is," Fast said, taking down some of the brandy without bothering to savor the heady fumes. "Enough to give you the blue spiders."

Alex said, as though confidentially, "Actually, I don't get it. At first, I thought the whole thing was crazy. People living for hundreds of years. I'm still not sure I'm not getting some kind of song and dance."

"Well, forget about that angle of it, friend. It's true all right. As a matter of fact, I'm one of them."

Alex pretended to stare at him in disbelief. "You mean you're one of these weirds who lives forever?"

"Yes. So far as I know, the only one in our organization. The others are taking the treatment but I don't need it. They haven't started you on it yet?"

"What treatment?"

"The prolongevity treatment, for Christ sake. It'll extend your life span indefinitely. That's what this whole thing is all about. The organization finally came through with all the answers."

"Like what?" Alex licked his lips as though anxious to be reassured.

"How would I know? I'm no damned scientist. They've been looking for the key for suspending senescence since the days of the alchemists, Roger Bacon and all the rest of them. Now they've found it. It was just a matter of time."

"And you're sure they'll give it to me?" Alex was hopeful.

Fast grinned at him, fox-like, there being a nasty

quality behind it. "Of course they will. Look, Germain, or whatever your real name is, they're honing down this organization to an edge. It's going to run like clockwork, see? It has to, or the whole thing will blow. There can be only a few hundred, at most, in on it. And they've got to be disciplined like no other organization in all history. There can't be any leaks, or the whole thing falls apart. We've got three basic groups. The scientists and their families, of course. We've got to have them to continually check, watch out for side effects and so forth. Then we've got to have the big shots, money and power, and, of course, their families. And third, we've got to have muscle. From Somerlott right on down to the field men, like us. I don't need the treatment, but you do and so do the others on this assignment. And you don't have to worry about the Chief doing you the dirty."

He leered, a caricature of a villain in a third rate movie. "Somerlott is going to need his goon squad from now on in. He's going to need dependable help like you and me, and Nick and Gino. Over and over again, as time goes by, situations will come up where he needs us. This enclave is possibly the largest gathering of emortals that's ever got together but even after we eliminate it, there'll be individuals spotted all over the world, maybe some of them grouped together like the bunch you handled in China. And as long as there are any of them at all, they're a danger to the organization. All they have to do is break cover and let the common herd know that prolongevity is possible and the shit will hit the fan."

The other came over so obnoxiously that it was

Alex Germain's every instinct to come to his feet and smash him on his long fox-like nose. And, from the side of his eyes, he could see Buda, stretched out on the floor watching them, felt the same way. Possibly the dog wasn't as smart as he seemed, as Cagliostro had told him, but he knew a wrong-o when he saw—or smelled—one.

"That's one of the things I don't understand," Alex said, pouring another shot for both of them. "What the devil's the point of this organization? Sure, I don't mind being on the in, but what's the ultimate objective?"

The other looked at him as though he was out of his mind. "Damn it, Germain, don't you see? We're in the catbird seat. Like no group, clique, class, caste, hierarchy, or whatever, in all history, we've got it made. The organization will continue, year after year, century after century, running the world. With the accumulated experience, mounting up every decade that goes by, in time we'll control every penny in the world and every position of power that makes any difference. Individuals will have to play it smart, pretending to die, and then surfacing somewhere else. They'll have to play it the same way I have, and Cohen and Hsu Fu and all the rest of the emortals, but in actuality they'll go on, behind the scenes, running everything. By Christ, man, don't you get the dream? We'll be the equivalent of gods."

"Yeah," Alex said, as though overwhelmed by it all. "And, you're right. They'll need people like us. Tough operators."

"You said it, friend. And they've got to give you prolongevity too. It doesn't make sense for the

Chief to recruit new field men every generation. Too much danger that somewhere along the line somebody would blow the whistle. It's a matter of you scratch my back and I'll scratch yours. We need him, and the organization, and he needs us. We've got it made."

Alex looked at him contemplatively. How had anybody managed to become this objectionable in only a few centuries? He had heard of Faust, or Faustus as he was sometimes called, as far back as when he, himself, had first become aware of his extended life span, and he'd never heard anything good about the bastard. And after all these years the other evidently hadn't developed beyond the second rate con man stage. On the face of it, the others, Ahasuerus, Hsu Fu, Nuscha and Lilith had mellowed with the centuries. As Lilith had said, Cohen was a gentleman. After all he had been through, how could he be anything else? But this ass?

He said, trying to project an air of camaraderie, "How in the devil did the organization contact you, Jack?"

The other was sneeringly amused. "They didn't. I contacted them. Thirty years ago, I saw the handwriting on the wall. It was all in the cards. A matter of time. So I kept in touch with the field. I read everything about gerontology that came up. I went to all their conventions. I kept my eyes open. Then, finally, something clicked and I knew it. Leif Mandlebaum and his team had made the breakthrough. I immediately got to him and told him my story." He made a mouth of modesty. "I let him know what had to be done. Christ, I was the one that pointed out to him that he had to get in touch with some operator such as the Chief and some of the big moneyed boys. I've been around for a long time, Germain. I know what side of my bread the butter's on."

At least three centuries, Alex thought, and the son-of-a-bitch hasn't even bothered to get an education. He speaks in cliches and sounds all but illiterate. He wondered what the other's I.Q. really was.

Jack Fast said, after looking at his wrist chronometer, "I've got a job to do now. No use ringing you in. You don't know the layout of the town or anything. And I don't need Gino and Nick yet, either. We'll all get together tomorrow, all of us, and play the final payoff. Gino has a get car, eh?"

Alex guessed at the idiomatic term. The other must mean a getaway vehicle. "Yes," he said. "A Volks mini-caravan."

"Great. That'll hold us all, complete with luggage. See you tomorrow, Alex." The pianist stood.

Alex arose too but it was Buda who saw the other back to the French windows and the terrace. The dog looked as though it was all he could do not to give Fast a quick nip in the bottom as he went.

When the hit man was gone, Alex sat there for a long time, trying to put it together. By purest chance, he had stumbled upon the foe and by the sheerest of luck he had managed to ingratiate himself with them. But just what did it all amount to? That Jack Fast, most likely with the assistance of the Beaumonts, had murdered Werner Gottlieb, he had no doubt whatsoever. And that they had plans against the whole enclave seemed as obvious as anything that could be. And matters were coming to a head with a rush. The arrival of the two men Lilith had spotted seemed all that had been waited for.

What other information had he picked up? Lief Mandlebaum, whose name as a gerontologist he was vaguely acquainted with, had seemingly made the breakthrough which resulted in prolongevity becoming a reality. And the Chief, Somerlott. Hadn't there been a General Somerlott heading the CIA, or one of the other cloak and dagger outfits, a few years ago? Alex didn't really keep up with government and politics much these days. He'd had enough of them in his earlier centuries.

But all summed up, if he'd read Jack Fast clearly, was the fact that prolongevity for everyman was now possible. And those who had made the discovery had decided to guard it for themselves, for fear that its revelation would dismember present day society. Guard it for themselves and utilize it to slowly seize power as power had never been taken over in history. And it would be the Somerlotts, the Jack Fasts, the Ginos and Nicks who would enforce it. He involuntarily squirmed at the idea.

But what was there to do now? He had to get in touch with Ahasuerus and Hsu Fu. Even more immediately, he had to find Cagliostro. Midnight, Giuseppe had said, damn it. He couldn't wait for twelve o'clock. It was already dark out but midnight was hours away. He and his sole comrade-in-arms had to equip themselves and begin taking measures.

How could he find Cagliostro? Lilith had said he had no phone.

He stood suddenly and made for the doorway, Buda following at a trot.

He headed for the office and found it empty and then went back into the little foyer and checked in the dining room. It was empty save for two of the enclave having their dinner.

Marcelo came up, menus in hand. "A table for one, Señor Germain?"

"Not now. Have you seen Señora Zavala?"

"I believe she went to Señor Cohen's house, sir. But I'm not sure."

Alex's mind raced. This was no time to be continuing his pose as a tourist who was getting the cold shoulder. However, he took a precaution, just on the off chance. He sighed and said, "It's a long life."

Marcelo looked puzzlement. "I suppose so, sir."

Alex said, "Look, you haven't seen Señor Balsamo, Giuseppe Balsamo, have you?"

"Not since earlier in the day when you had lunch with him in the small dining room."

"I'd like to find him. Where does he live?"

The maitre d' hesitated but then said, "Just down the street a bit. If you turn right as you leave the hotel, you cross over two streets and the third is Calle de Jesus. Turn right, there, and his house is the second to the right. I believe the number is 48."

Alex shrugged it off. "Ah, the devil with it. He'll probably turn up later tonight. Thanks Marcelo." He turned and headed for his room, the dog trotting ahead.

He barricaded his door with the same heavy chair as before and got his dark clothing from his bag and donned it. He brought forth the black silk handkerchief and flashlight Hsu Fu had returned to him and stuck them in a pocket of the pants. He then took up his knife and sheath and placed them in his belt, under the dark shirt.

Alex looked at the dog thoughtfully. He said, "I don't know if I should take you along or not. Anybody seeing you would know it was me you were with."

The hound wagged at him hopefully and hung out his tongue. He was obviously gung ho.

"On the other hand, except for this pigsticker, you're the only weapon I have. You'd better come." He headed for the terrace.

Up on the roof, he started for the adjoining building, once occupied by Buda's master. But then came to a halt. A figure had emerged from the stairway which led down into the area of the hotel rooms and suites. A figure swathed in black, from head to foot. It startled when he could be made out in his own dark clothing.

"Good evening, Fay," he said gently.

"I . . . I . . . Darling, it's you!" She came closer, breathing heavily.

He said, "Fay, it's no good. I'm not right for this. I'm not what you want."

"Oh, yes. Oh, yes you are, darling. I need you. I want you so badly." Her voice was raw with sex.

"Look, honey, what you need is a psychiatrist. Some of the enclave must be doctors. Aren't there any psychiatrists, or at least psychologists? You need counseling."

"I need love!" she whined, grabbing for him. He stepped back but she had one arm, fiercely. "You don't understand. I must have love. I must be loved, taken, possessed."

He shook his head, feeling terrible, feeling miserably depressed.

"I'm sorry, Fay. I'm not available. Even if I wanted to, I couldn't stand your pace."

She pressed her mature body up against him so that he could feel through cloak and nightgown the fullness of her breasts, the nipples hard, the warmth of her hips and her pubic mound. Her heavy mouth was half open.

"But I have to have you, darling."

"I'm afraid there's someone else, Fay."

She glared up into his face and bared her perfect teeth. "It's that bitch, Lilith. That mealy mouthed Lilith. Darling, she can't give you what I can. I'll teach you a thousand methods of making love. I'll smother you in the act of passion. She knows nothing, compared to me."

He disentangled from her, trying to keep from being rough.

"Sorry, Fay."

"But you don't understand," she moaned urgently. "I must have love or I grow old. Wrinkles come to my face, my skin becomes dry and gray. I lose my energy. I become old. I become . . . afraid of death."

He pushed her from him.

She shook her head negatively, woefully, unbelievingly, but slowly turned and headed back in the direction from which she had come, her motion now a dragging rather than the graceful glide.

When she had disappeared into the dark of the night, Alex Germain closed his eyes in pain. Finally, he said, "Come along, boy."

They descended into the depths of the Gottlieb house, he refraining from switching on the lights but utilizing his small flashlight. The place was empty, as he had been sure it would be.

At the front door, he opened it a crack and peered up and down. At this point, above all he didn't want to come up against Jack Fast or the two Beaumonts, now to be recognized as belonging to the ranks of the foe.

But the street was clear. He stepped quickly out and closed the door behind him. As before, the streets of San Raphael were poorly lit at night. He made his way along them furtively, sticking to the shadows. Buda caught the feeling of the game and walked along the side of the walls, as close to them as possible.

Alex whispered to the dog, "If we meet Jack Fast out here, we try to eliminate him, bring him down. You understand, boy?"

"Yiss." The dog's tongue emerged and he panted slightly. He obviously approved of the idea.

The third street was Calle de Jesus, Hey-Zeus, as pronounced in Spanish. They turned right and Marcelo had been correct, the second house was Number 48. As they reached it, he could see somebody approaching from up the street, coming from the direction of the center of town. He hurriedly tried the heavy iron doorknob and mercifully it gave. They slipped inside and he closed the iron studded door behind them.

There were no lights. Damn it. Cagliostro wasn't

here. Where could he be? At Cohen's? There seemed to be some kind of a meeting going on at the town presidente's home. He kicked himself for not finding out where the enclave leader lived. The address would have been in the phone book, assuming there was a Celaya directory in the hotel's office. Or, he could have asked Marcelo, though hardly without arousing the head waiter's suspicion. Why should the tourist, Alex Germain, be seeking out San Raphael's mayor? Damn it again. He should have suggested that Marcelo be included among the few that knew his real identity.

He brought out his flashlight and flicked it around the entrada which was almost identical to that of Gottlieb's house and was a smaller edition of the entrance to the Sierra Nevada. By the looks of it, the living room was off to the right, before you emerged into the inevitable patio. He headed for it. Possibly, he could find where Cagliostro hid his cache of arms and equip himself.

As they entered the room, Buda growled in low alarm.

"What is it, boy? Somebody here?" His right hand went to his knife. He stretched his left hand out far to the side with the light. If anyone shot for it, they wouldn't hit his body.

But there was no one present. No one alive. The room was in a shambles. Torn apart. It came to him that he wasn't going to find his old friend's arms supply. Someone else had come first. Had come first and had left the adventurer Count Alessandro Cagliostro with the results of the last event of violence in which he would ever participate.

For Giuseppe Balsamo was sprawled on the floor, at least a dozen bullet wounds stitched up across belly and chest.

Interlude

When the communicator's screen lit up with the general's face, he said, "Yes, sir."

"Well, give me your report, mister, damn it."

"The report is progress, Chief. The emortals had stored their small arsenal in the home of this Cagliostro. We broke in, eliminated him and confiscated every weapon they had. They're now defenseless, even if any of them had the training for combat, and they haven't. Cagliostro was the only one who had ever seen action, and, like I said, we liquidated him."

"Have Nick Terry and Gino Bova shown up with the hardware and your getaway vehicle? They have all instructions. You will have to drive only twenty miles to rendezvous with the aircraft which will return you to the States."

"Yes, sir. They arrived just a short time ago. And Alex Germain, too."

The other's craggy, military face went stonier still. "Who?"

"Alex Germain. I assume that's not his real name. He's the operative who used to work under you in the Orient. Did in the enclave in China."

The general glared at him. "Are you out of your ever-fucking mind, mister? What enclave in China? The only operatives I've sent into San Raphael are first you, then Martha Malloy and that kill-happy boy friend of hers, Bill Shirey, and just these last couple of days Nick Terry and Gino Bova with the hardware you'll need. Now who in the hell is this Germain?"

His lips went white and there was temerity in his voice. "I . . . I thought I remembered the name. But it was ridiculous. I should have known better. But now I realize who he is. He's the Comte de Saint-Germain. But, well, he had the passwords and knew your name and seemingly all about this operation."

"Mister, you'd better start making sense. Just who in the Christ is the Comte de Saint-Germain?"

"In the past, he was one of the most dangerous men in Europe. Among other things, he master-minded the overthrow of the Czar and Catherine the Great's taking over power in St. Petersburg. He's one of these centuries old emortals, Chief."

The other's voice held rage. "So are you, you damned incompetent. And I'm beginning to suspect you're senile. Liquidate him! And all of them! Those are your orders, mister, and if they aren't fulfilled, you'd better damn well head for the hills yourself!"

Chapter 6

No case has yet been presented for an average life of 100 or 150 years being significantly better than one of 75 years. More of the same is not, by itself, a good argument ... Until some good reasons have been presented why a longer life per se is good, as distinguished from a long life where life's evils have been minimized as far as possible, there is no public policy case to be made for the investment of one cent in efforts to extend it.
—Daniel Callahan
"Natural Death and Public Policy"
Life Span, edited by Robert Veatch

1.

The same feeling of horror that had washed over Alex Germain when he had come upon the mutilated body of Werner Gottlieb was with him again. His eyes were sick. "Ai, Giuseppe," he muttered.

"After all the years. After all you've been through. To wind up in a small ruin of a town in the backwaters of Mexico."

Buda had approached the body, stifflegged, and sniffed at it. Nothing was sure in the world of the canine until it was smelled. He moaned deep in his throat and turned and looked up at Alex questioningly.

Alex shook his head. "There's nothing we can do, boy. The same enemies who killed your master have now murdered Cagliostro. They move quickly. I should have known when Fast told me he had something to do tonight that it would be on the order of this. I was an idiot not to have tried to finish him off then and there. Then Giuseppe and I together could have taken on the others, two by two."

Buda suddenly stiffened and pointed to the door, his right paw slightly off the floor and tucked back as though he was performing his duties as a hunting dog.

Alex hissed, "What is it, boy?"

Now he could hear what the Vizsla had already detected. The sounds of someone at the front door. He quickly doused the small beam of his flashlight.

His knife was suddenly in hand. He stepped to one side of the living room doorway. Buda slithered over to take his stance at the other side, the stiff short hair at the back of his neck ruffled. They could hear someone entering. Seemingly, it was but a single person.

Light suddenly flooded the room. The switch must have been at the doorway on the outside of the chamber.

Hsu Fu came through the door, his wizened face expressing anxiety. His eyes hit upon the fallen body before he noticed Alex or the animal.

"Caglio . . ." he began to blurt.

Alex Germain returned his knife to its sheath. "He's dead," he said emptily.

The Chinese turned to him in dismay. "Comte Saint-Germain! What has happened?"

Alex spread his hands. "I arrived only moments before you. In fact, I saw you coming down the street as I entered the house. Giuseppe was to give me arms from the enclave's arsenal. I found him like this. I suspect the enemy has confiscated what equipment he had. What are you doing here?"

Hsu Fu temporarily ignored the question and went to a large Colonial period santo painting of a crucifixion scene which hung above the fireplace. He slid the aged painting to one side, evidently it being on some kind of roller arrangement. Behind was a large cavity, a compartment set into the supposed chimney. It looked empty. The Chinese reached in and felt around to emerge with two cartridge boxes.

He said in his mild voice, "Only the members of the enclave knew where the guns were hidden. They're all gone." He looked down at the boxes he held. "This is all that is left."

Which was quite obvious to Alex Germain.

The ancient looking Chinese said, "What am I doing here? Why I came for Cagliostro. He had no phone. And then I was going to pick you up. We are holding a small emergency meeting at the home of David Cohen. We have decided that the enclave must convene in its entirety and decide upon what must be done. However, if there is a traitor, or more, among us, then he would immediately know. Lilith has told us about the two new strangers in San Raphael. If they were informed we were meeting, they would have us all together. What is the so clever American term? Sitting ducks.''

Alex nodded to that. He said, "I've got some things I want to talk about with you but we'd better not stay here. For whatever reason, the killers might come back. Let's go up to Gottlieb's house. Nobody would expect us to be there. And there's a phone."

The other made no objection to that and they left, the Chinese switching off the light as they departed the living room, leaving the sprawled body behind.

Alex opened the front door carefully and the dog slid out before them peering alertly up and down the street. He wagged his stub of a tail to indicate all was clear.

They hurried to Calle Hospicio and then up it, making no effort to hide themselves, it being out of the question that three figures could move without being spotted, particularly since Hsu Fu was not attired in the black clothing Alex affected.

At the doorway to the late professor's house they again looked up and down sharply but at this time of night the streets were barren. The door was still unlocked from Alex's earlier passage and they entered.

In the living room, Hsu Fu switched on the lights and when Alex looked askance said, "The light can't be detected from the street. As you see, there are no windows."

He slumped into a chair, as though weak from the experience of finding Cagliostro dead. Alex found a place across from him and the dog sank at his feet.

The Chinese said, in his small gentle voice, "In actuality, I never took to our so unfortunate Cagliostro. I do not know why." He shook his head. "But he was a man of good will, no matter what his earlier life might have been. Time, I suppose, mellows us all." He looked at Alex ruefully. "For that matter, my first impressions of you were not the best. Why?" His thin shoulders shrugged. "Perhaps I am mistrustful of emortals that do not attempt to efface themselves, as most of us do."

Alex allowed himself a sour chuckle. "You wound me sorely. It's taken me a long time to develop my present cover and front. In the far past, I projected myself as an arrogant nobleman. Today, I am supposedly an easy-going freelance newsman. There have been other characters I assumed in between. Sometimes I wonder if I have a real personality, somewhere beneath all the false fronts I have assumed down through the centuries."

He took a deep breath. "To what extent are the police armed and are you in a position to take over such weapons?"

The other looked at him. "David and I control the police completely. There are eight of them in all. In the police armory there are eight revolvers and two carbines."

"Nothing else? No shotguns, no riot guns? I suppose no submachine gun?"

The question obviously did not make sense to the other who said, "San Raphael is possibly the most peaceful village in Mexico. Usually, our police do not even carry their guns when on duty."

Alex hid his dismay but he had actually not

expected any other response. He said, "The two
men who came today are most likely equipped
with the latest in terrorist arms, undoubtedly including submachine guns, and most likely such
items as grenades. We couldn't possibly put up a
fight and even if we could, such a shoot-out would
be beyond even Cohen hushing up. It would draw
not only Mexican attention but worldwide and the
enclave would be revealed. There is just no way of
fighting and coming out ahead. There's only one
answer. The community's got to split up. Now.
Tonight. We'll have to head out in all directions.
Each man and woman for themselves."

The Chinese said, "David, Ursula, Lilith and I
had come to about the same conclusion in our
meeting tonight. But, as I told you, we fear to call
a meeting because if there is a traitor among us,
and obviously there is, he too would receive the
notice of the gathering and could betray us to
these new killers."

"Actually," Alex said urgently, "there is no need
for such a meeting. Just send out the word for
everybody to get out of town before dawn. Get on
the phone to Cohen and tell him to start spreading
the word."

The small, seemingly withered man was shaking
his head. "You don't understand. David is in no
position to give such orders, to disperse the whole
community. His voice, or my own humble one, has
no more authority than that of any other member
of our group. We govern ourselves, if that is the
term, something like the old New England Town
Meetings. It takes the whole community to make
such a decision as this."

Alex groaned. "Nothing like democracy," he said.

"But how can we meet?" the other said. "The foe will immediately know and attack, if that is what they have in mind and it is obvious that they do. Already they have murdered two of our number."

Alex rubbed his left hand over his mouth. "No," he said. "That's not the immediate worry. We have until tomorrow. Your spy in the enclave is Faust. Jack Fast. The two supposed Texans, the Beaumonts, are also part of his killer team. By pure luck, I managed to stumble upon the fact and put myself over as still another gunman sent by their chief, somebody named Somerlott. Thus far, the three of them haven't gotten in contact with the two newcomers, who are probably named Gino and Nick. Fast told me that we'd all get together tomorrow and lay the final plans for finishing off the enclave. So the thing to do now is get in touch with our whole group and call the meeting."

Hsu Fu was staring at him as though frustrated.

"No. Wait a minute," Alex said, thinking. "We can't take a chance using the phone. Fast and his gang probably have at their disposal the most sophisticated equipment they need. There's a good chance that some of our phones are tapped, especially Cohen's and especially any in the hotel. You'll have to call the meeting by personally contacting each member."

"But . . . but that's impossible, if we only have tonight. There are almost two hundred of us scattered all about the town."

Alex was impatient. "Simple enough," he said, coming to his feet. "Go back to Cohen, Nuscha and Lilith and explain the situation. Then all four of you start out to spread the word of the gathering. Have each person you tell go out in turn and give notice to two others before heading for the hotel. In an hour or so, all of the enclave will be notified."

The Chinese stood too. "Yes, so obvious. A geometric progression. It didn't occur to me. This one is a fool. I shall start immediately." He headed for the door.

Alex said, "I'll go to the hotel and tell Marcelo to prepare for the meeting."

He didn't bother to mention the fact that if Jack Fast was there he was going to have to eliminate the traitor. If possible. The man was undoubtedly armed and with more than a handmade knife at that.

But as he entered the Sierra Nevada he couldn't hear the tinkle of Fast's piano, nor were the Beaumonts seated at their favorite table in the patio. He went over to the bar and darted a quick look in but no one was there save Paco who was polishing glasses.

Alex went on to the dining room. The Beaumonts weren't there either. At this hour there were but four diners, all of them the usual seemingly elderly members of the enclave. Marcelo and his two waiters looked bored and as though they were only waiting for the handful of customers to finish so that they could clean up and call it a night.

Alex remained in the foyer until he was able to catch the head waiter's eye and give him the nod. Marcelo approached looking as though he didn't appreciate the lateness of Alex's appearance.

He said, "A table for one, Señor Germain? I am afraid that the Señora isn't available in the kitchen and it is about to close. However, perhaps a sandwich and glass of . . ."

Alex said urgently, "Listen, Marcelo. I'm one of

you. Cohen and several of the others already know it."

The other nodded, accepting the fact immediately. "I was beginning to suspect so. The way you . . ."

Alex interrupted him. "I'll have to tell you this quickly. The enclave is in the clutch. Cagliostro has been killed and the arms cache stolen. Jack Fast is our traitor. And the Beaumonts are with him."

Marcelo nodded. "I had begun to suspect them, too. Earlier today the man forgot and left his glasses on a table. I looked closely at them before returning them. The lenses were of plain glass. They weren't spectacles at all."

"Have you seen Jack Fast or the Beaumonts?"

"Not for some hours. What's happening?"

"Two more gunmen came into town this afternoon. That makes five of them in all. We suspect their intention is to massacre the whole community. It's been decided to convene here and decide what to do."

Marcelo nodded. "I'll dismiss the waiters and the kitchen staff and set up the conference room. Anything else . . . Alex?"

He shook his head. "I can't think of anything. You'd better tell the four, in there in the dining room, about the meeting. Look, is that conference room soundproof?"

"Yes."

"And light-proof? That is, when the window drapes are drawn?"

"Yes. And I can see what you're leading to. I'll stay out here. We have a bell arrangement. If Fast comes in—I never did like that damn sneak—I'll press a button here and it will ring in the hall to warn you. I'll also do my best to stick a steak knife in his ribs before he realizes I'm on to him."

Alex hesitated, not quite knowing what to do at this point.

Marcelo said, his face straight, "If I am not mistaken, Lilith is waiting for you. Ah, up in your room."

"Thanks," he said. "Come along, Buda."

Alex ascended the stairs, the dog leading the way, and opened the door to find the girl—girl? that was a laugh—in the same chair she'd been in the night before when he'd returned from prowling the hospital.

He said quickly, "You haven't seen Hsu Fu? I thought you were at Cohen's."

"I just returned. I had to see you. What in the hell's wrong, Alex?"

"It's all right. Hsu Fu and the rest of them can start the ball rolling. Honey, Cagliostro's dead. And the enclave arsenal has been looted. The community's going to meet in the conference hall and decide tonight what to do. Fast and the Beaumonts are the enemy. They're going to get together tomorrow with the new hit men to make the final plans regarding us. We've got until then, no longer."

She had come to her feet upon his arrival. Now she closed her eyes and said in ultimate weariness, "Oh, Goddamn." The expletive, coming from her, still seemed out of character.

He took her in his arms, knowing the gesture to be meaningless. He had no assurance to give.

He said, "What was it you had to see me about?"

"Our plans. Cohen, Hsu Fu and Ursula are about of the same mind, though she has some misgivings.

The enclave will have to be abandoned. Hsu Fu and David are quite sure that when put to a vote the community will concur. But there are other questions to be settled. Meanwhile we . . . that is, you and I . . ."

He pushed her away from his embrace and put his hands on her shoulders, looking truly into her eyes. He said, "So far as I am concerned, Lilith, from now on we're a team. No matter what happens, we'll stick together." He looked down at Buda who had stretched out on the floor and was watching them with interest. "Including our dog, of course."

Buda wagged the stub of tail and lolled out his tongue for a couple of pants of heartfelt agreement.

"Yes, of course," she said, her voice low. "Darling, have you ever had a . . . a permanent arrangement with a fellow emortal before?"

He shook his head. "No. Never. My, uh, permanent arrangements have always been with women living the usual life expectancy. It was too much. I had given up so-called permanent arrangements."

"And so had I," she nodded. The sides of her mouth turned down in her infinitely sad smile. "You marry a man when you are both seemingly about thirty years of age. A mere thirty years later and he is sixty and, aside from all other complications, it becomes increasingly difficult for him to understand why he is aging but, in spite of all I do, I cannot hide that I am not. Ten years later and he is an old man and all that can be done is leave him. To remain is out of the question and certainly no kindness."

"Yes, I know," he said.

"No matter how much love there once might

have been, there is nothing to do but disappear from the scene, leaving him to his sorrow and taking your own with you."

"Yes, I know," he agreed again. The scene was too mutually painful and there was nothing more to be said. He released her and went to a window.

Down below, in the patio, members of the enclave were beginning to stream in.

"Hsu Fu and Cohen must have gotten a move on," he muttered. "Oh, Christ, I hope Fast and the Beaumonts don't turn up."

"You don't have to worry about them."

He turned and looked at her in surprise. "Why not? That's our big worry. But there evidently is simply no other place to meet."

"I saw the Beaumonts going up to their suite not long ago. They didn't eat supper. He seemed stinking assed drunk. At least, she was kind of helping him along."

"But how about Fast?"

"I saw him only a few minutes ago with Fay. They were obviously on their way to her place. They've had an off-again, on-again affair going since first he arrived. I don't think he's quite up to her demands but every week or so he tries again. He's a little weasel of a bastard, you know."

He grunted at that. "Yes, I know. I suppose we ought to go on below. I haven't met any of these people at all, except you few around the hotel."

2.

Down on the first floor he said to her, "You go on to the assembly room. I'll join you in a few minutes. I have to see Marcelo."

"All right, darling."

He looked after her for a moment. The infinite grace of her. She moved-with the erect confidence of a queen. But then, of course, once she had been. He doubted her Nefertiti story not at all. It came to him that of the nearly two hundred citizens of the enclave perhaps more than one had, in his time, almost as unbelievable stories to tell. In a millennium almost anything can happen. What was it that someone had mentioned about Hsu Fu? That he had helped hide Montezuma's treasure?

He went out into the patio, seeking the maitre d' and spotted him in the street doorway looking anxiously up and down Calle Hospicio. Enclave members continued to stream through the doors talking in whispers among themselves, heading for the conference room. There was considerable tension in the air but somehow it was an experienced tension and Alex Germain realized that all of them, all of them, had been in the clutch before and most, time and time again.

He came up and said to Marcelo, "It's better than we could have hoped for. Lilith saw the Beaumonts going up to their room. He was evidently smashed. Probably in anticipation of what's going to happen tomorrow, or so they think."

"But Fast? He's the ringleader, isn't he?"

"So he told me. But he's a blowhard. Don't underestimate our friends Bill and Martha. In spite of that front they've been putting on, they're probably more dangerous than the legendary Bonnie and Clyde. Lilith also spotted Fast and Fay Morgan heading for her home."

Marcelo looked relieved. "Good. She'll screw him flat. It'll take him half of tomorrow to recover."

Alex said, "Warn everybody who comes in to keep their voices low. We wouldn't want the Beaumonts to hear this gathering."

He turned and headed back for the conference room.

There were already about fifty persons. Some participating in setting up the chairs to face the podium. Some already seated. Some standing around in small groups chattering low and anxiously. Lilith he spotted sitting quietly alone in the first row.

Cohen, Hsu Fu and Nuscha had all arrived. They had evidently each notified two enclave members and then hurried back to the hotel to help supervise the organization of the meeting. Alex came up to them and explained the latest developments, that is that Fast and the Beaumonts were accounted for. They were, on the face of it, greatly relieved.

Ursula snorted. "At least that bed-happy wench is being of some use to the community. I hope she gives him a dose of clap. The way she spreads herself around, it's almost unbelievable that she hasn't picked up every disease in the manual."

"My dear," Cohen said in mild protest. "After all, Fay is one of our community and, in actuality, should be here for this meeting."

Alex rolled his eyes upward as though appealing to higher powers. "Great. That's all we need," he said. "For somebody to go and drag her out of bed with Faust and tell her a meeting is on."

"I am afraid you jest," Hsu Fu murmured.

Alex looked about the hall which was rapidly filling up.

Something came to him and he said to Cohen, "No Orientals, save Hsu Fu here? No Africans?"

Cohen said, "How would we contact them? Undoubtedly, they exist. Actually, two of us are American blacks, but hardly a hundred percent Africans, if there are any full blooded Africans in the United States, save those most recently come over. We had a Japanese American but he died at the age of only a hundred and fifty or so."

Alex looked at Hsu Fu.

The Chinese said, "Long before the Christian era, in China we had an enclave something like this, though smaller. We conducted experiments in prolongevity, as far as we could in view of our early equipment and inadequate knowledge. It became an 'in' thing among the intellectuals and then among the aristocracy. In fact, the Emperor became obsessed with the idea and we grew afraid that we emortals would be seized and put to the torture to disclose our supposed secrets."

Alex said, "I'm acquainted with the story in the Shih Chi about the supposed blessed islands located in the Eastern Ocean and how a certain Hsu Fu was sent to find them. Wasn't it about 220 B.C.?"

"Yes. And, of course, I am the same Hsu Fu. The story in the Shih Chi account is somewhat inaccurate. It is true that our group of emortals cozened Emperor Chin Shih Huang Ti into letting us take a junk to explore and find the islands of supposed emortality. Instead, of course, we continued on and eventually disembarked near present day Acapulco."

"A whole group of you?" Alex said. "Where are the rest today?"

The small Chinese looked at him sadly. "One by one they died over the centuries. The last, a woman, only some three hundred years ago."

Alex stared at him. "But why didn't you bring Meso-America the advances that had already taken place in China? The wheel, bronze, iron, gunpowder . . ."

The Chinese was wry. "Perhaps I did influence them a very small bit. The Olmecs, the first of the advanced Mexican cultures, were in their infancy when we arrived. But the wheel? Without domesticated animals? Iron and bronze? I was a scholar, not a metal worker. Even today, I would not recognize iron ore if I saw it, nor would I know how to extract it, if I did. Bronze? I vaguely know it is an amalgamation of copper and tin. But in what proportions? Besides, this stupid one wouldn't know tin if he saw it. Gunpowder? Yes, it was first invented in China but for use in fireworks and, once again, I had no idea of how to make it. Besides, primitive people such as the Mexicans live by ritual and taboo, they do not welcome change. And if you attempt to introduce it, you become conspicuous. And an emortal must never become conspicuous."

The room was continuing to fill but obviously all were not present as yet.

Alex looked at Cohen. "Everyone seems to use the term emortal. It's new to me."

"Indeed?" Cohen said. "It is a valid word to describe us. In logic, the symbol of the universal negative is the letter 'e'. So, the word emortal would indicate the negative of mortal."

The balance of the community came in a rush and with surprising order found chairs and settled down.

Cohen said to Alex, "Would you join me on the dais? I usually open the meetings. Lilith is our senior member but she is somewhat of retiring disposition and defers to me as second eldest."

"All right," Alex said, following him, not knowing what the other had in mind. The dog trotted after them and took his position lying on the floor next to the podium, his gold-red eyes scanning the audience.

There were two chairs behind the speaker's stand and Alex took one of them as Cohen rapped with his knuckles for attention.

The audience, Alex realized, projected itself somewhat differently than they did in public, under the eyes of strangers or the hired help of the Sierra Nevada. Elderly, their get-up and especially attire might proclaim them, but here, divorced from outsiders, their emortal youth showed through. They were more animated, sharper, quicker of movement. Largely, their eyes were on him, questioningly.

Small to the point of being delicate, David Cohen might be but he made a self-possessed, positive chairman.

"Fellow emortals," he said, "our community is in ultimate danger. Never have we been faced with such potential disaster. Tonight, we must make decisions that can never be reversed."

There was a stirring throughout the hall but silence prevailed. The youngest among them was well over the century mark and they had learned discipline.

Cohen said, "We have a new member of the enclave among us tonight, in the past once known as the Comte de Saint-Germain, today as Alex Germain. He has been a man of action, as so few of the rest of us, if any, save for the late Giuseppe Balsamo, Cagliostro."

When he used the term 'late' there was a drawing in of air throughout the assemblage.

Cohen went on. "I am going to introduce Alex Germain, who will inform you of our present situation of which he is more aware than I am myself." He turned and said, "Alex, if you will."

Alex stood, even as the chairman took a seat.

There was no applause, only complete attention.

He said, "I'll go through no preliminaries about being glad to be here and that sort of thing. I'm not glad to be here. And I rather doubt that anybody else is. In my opinion, this enclave is going to be forced to disband within hours or most, if not all, of us will be massacred."

He paused for a moment to allow them to digest that.

Alex went on. "Briefly, the situation is this. Scientists under the gerontologist Lief Mandlebaum have made the breakthrough we have all more or less been expecting. Evidently confronted with problems to which they could see no answers, if their discoveries were released, they turned for advice and support to two of the most opportunistic, elements which our tired and sad world provides, the international power elite and the would-be men on horseback, so well portrayed, years ago, by George Orwell in his *1984* and by Aldous Huxley in *Brave New World*."

He looked out over them. Tears were in the eyes of many, men as well as women. And he could only realize that for the greater number of them this seemingly secure community was the only real sanctuary they had ever known down through the centuries.

He said, "It becomes obvious that they see in us, true natural emortals, a thorn in the side of their plans which they cannot stand. Their scheme is to keep their artificial means of achieving prolongevity for themselves and to utilize it to gain domination over all Earth. To keep such a secret from the masses of humanity they cannot tolerate that we might reveal ourselves and let it be known that a longer life span is possible for the species. A certain Somerlott, a former general, I believe, in one of the many cloak and dagger espionage-counter-espionage organizations which have proliferated during the past century, has been given the task of reducing us."

Alex wound it up. "That's about it. I'm of the opinion that we should take all measure to abandon San Raphael and scatter. However, I am told that according to your usage such steps as this must be debated and voted upon. I'll turn the meeting back to our chairman. David?"

Alex resumed his seat as Cohen took over again.

"Does anyone wish to open the discussion? Frankly, I concur with Alex Germain."

Ursula Zavala, who was seated with Lilith and Hsu Fu in the first row of chairs, stood and turned to face the assemblage.

She said, "I don't believe we should rush into this. Perhaps we can come to terms with Lief Mandlebaum and the other scientists who have made the breakthrough and those with whom they are affiliated. Much of the stand they are taking is valid. The world is in no position to accept the disruption involved in an expansion of the life span for all. The population explosion is already a rampant problem. The disruption of Social Security and all pensions would shake most societies. And if ultimately we ceased having children evolution would end. If we can come to terms with this group we can continue, along with them, to live as emortals, but the balance of the species will continue at the present life expectancy. Mandlebaum and the others should welcome us to their ranks. We can offer ourselves for experimentation. Although they have discovered some method of prolonging life, undoubtedly they have a great deal more to learn. Prolongevity is in its infancy. We do not even know to what extent they have been successful. Can they extend life for fifty years, a century, or have they already discovered true emortality, such as to be witnessed in Lilith, David and Hsu Fu? Possibly they would welcome us if we took oaths not to reveal ourselves to the public. In return for our silence and cooperation in their experiments, they would let us alone."

Without rising from his chair, Alex called out, "Nuscha, you dreamer, you. There are too many of us for them to trust. How could they be sure that one might not renege and blow the whistle? No, they can't take the chance. And we can't trust them to keep their promise even if they made an agreement with us. They've proven their ruthlessness in their killing of the innocent Professor Gottlieb and of Cagliostro."

A woman half way down the hall raised her hand and Cohen acknowledged her.

She said, "The argument about the disruption of

Social Security and other pensions is of little importance. Pensions were established to provide for the elderly when they became no longer fit to work. Given emortality for all, so that each remained in youth or in early middle age, such as ourselves, there would be no need for pensions."

A man seated directly behind Hsu Fu, who wore a white smock came to his feet. Alex vaguely recalled having seen him in the lobby of the hospital.

He said, "This so called danger of population explosion is nonsense. Our population is doubling every forty years now simply because women are having more than two children apiece. If you lowered this to but two children per woman the population would eventually stabilize, no matter how long each person lived. Of course, it would increase linearly at first, as people failed to die, but there would be no exponential population explosion as long as each woman bore but two children." He sat down abruptly.

Someone a few rows back was recognized by Cohen and said, "This has been discussed before. To enforce a birth rate of no more than two children for each woman would require world government, and that, in turn, would mean the overthrow of every present government, including those of both the West and East. It doesn't seem very possible."

David Cohen put in a word there. "Personally, I am in favor of eventual world government but I see no immediate need for it in this case. The prolongevity treatment could be put in the hands of a world body, say the Reunited Nations. Every individual in the world, upon having given birth to the limit of two children, could then be sterilized. If sterilization was not accepted, then that person would not receive prolongevity treatment. It would be as simple as that."

Hsu Fu, after getting the chairman's recognition, turned and faced the meeting and said, "It comes to this person that David Cohen's program would answer another question raised by Señora Zavala. With two children allowed each female of our species, evolution would not be ended. It might possibly be slowed a bit, but not ended. Today, in India, Africa, Latin America, families of ten children are not unknown. Most of them die before reaching adulthood, of starvation or diseases brought on by malnutrition. With all these subjects, Mother Nature muddles through, in her efforts to achieve evolution. However, in the future, evolution will be taken into the laboratory and we will make strides in a matter of years that Nature would be hard put to accomplish in thousands. The two children per woman would be ample."

Someone down the hall called out, "Think of the great advances the race could make if all were granted emortality. Imagine, instead of living less than a century, a Beethoven, Newton or Shelley living for a thousand years."

And someone else called, "Yes. Or a Tamerlane, Stalin or Jack the Ripper."

Laughter rippled through the conference room, and Cohen, chuckling himself, rapped his knuckles on the stand before him for order.

Ursula was on her feet again, fiddling nervously with her sole earring, her face set in stubbornness. She said, "Are we sure the human race wants emortality? Are we sure that living to the age of two hundred or even a thousand is more desirable than living to 75? It has been argued that a full life can be had in 75 years. Is simply more of the same actually wanted?"

Another, in the very rear of the hall, raised hand and was recognized.

She said strongly, "It should be up to the individual to decide. We here, tonight, some two hundred of us, have opted for prolongevity. Others, born like ourselves, natural emortals, have decided against a greater life span and have suicided. I, myself, had a twin brother who lived for three centuries and then threw himself from a cliff. So must all the rest of us decide, the whole race. Let those who would survive do so, let those who would rather not, refuse the treatment. It is a decision not up to us to make. Senescence has been conquered, what to do with this new knowledge is not in our hands."

The man in the smock was on his feet again. "We could keep this going all night. But each minute that passes increases the danger that Faust and his gang will be upon us and prevent our escape. I make a motion that the enclave disband and each of us find hiding. And that in exactly one month we surface and proclaim the truth. The enemy is largely in control of the media but not all of it. And, besides, two hundred voices are too many to quell. Attempts will be made to silence us but the message will out that Lief Mandlebaum and his team have made the great breakthrough in gerontology."

"Second!" someone called.

Cohen said, "There will be a show of hands." And shortly afterwards, "The motion is carried all but unanimously. The question now becomes, where shall we go? You are all acquainted with the fact that we have an alternative location in Kenya. Long years ago Hsu Fu and I bought up the area. It would be possible for us to scatter at this point and then, later, reform there."

But Alex stood and said, "May I speak, Mr. Chairman?"

He looked out over the hall. "In the past, San Raphael was one thing. No one was especially looking for you. But now we are confronted by one of the most powerful and desperate organizations the world has ever seen. If we attempted to gather again, it would be only a short time before the enemy was upon us. Scattered, and with our long experience in concealing ourselves, some, if not most, will survive and perhaps something will develop in the future, near or far, that will enable us to seek each other out again and resume an emortal community of compatible people."

Cohen said sadly, "I am afraid that Alex is correct. I suggest the following. There are some cars among us which we will share. I will also commandeer the school buses, the hospital ambulance and the two garbage trucks. Half of us will go to Celaya, half to Queretero in the other direction. When they arrive at those points, they will separate, some to take train or bus south to Mexico City, and then on, some to head north for the border. Some may head east or west to the coasts, there to take ship or aircraft for whatever destination they choose. I strongly suggest that you do not remain in groups of more than two. As Alex has pointed out, the enemy is ruthless and will do everything to seek us out and silence us. Take as little luggage as possible. Aside from the fact that we don't have the room in our limited number of vehicles, it would prove an impediment in your flight. However, I suppose most of us have been through this before, that is, the need to abandon one's property in order to flee to maintain freedom.

"We have on hand, for just such an emergency as this, ample funds. Those of you who require them, check with me or Hsu Fu. We have pesos, dollars, Common Europe francs and marks, and Japanese yen, according to where you plan to go. Most of you carry adequate papers. If you don't, check with me and we'll see you are equipped with passports or whatever else needed from our secret documents room here in the hotel."

"What are you to do, David?" someone called.

The delicate little man shook his head. "I shall remain here in San Raphael in hiding. Perhaps in a few months conditions will so change that I will be able to emerge again. Perhaps not. Perhaps I will be caught. However, I am long tired of wandering. San Raphael is my final home."

"And mine," Hsu Fu said softly. "This humble one will also remain."

Of a sudden, Alex Germain felt the eyes upon him again. The eyes that had followed him so questioningly in the square. But now there was change. Now they were malevolent, evil overpowering.

3.

It was, of course, Jack Fast, though his face was masked in a latest model gas mask, a filter arrangement over the mouthpiece so that speech was possible. He stood in the doorway, his legs spread and in his hands was an Israeli Uzi parabellum submachine gun. Over his shoulders were slung two canvas sacks undoubtedly carrying additional magazines of 32 rounds each. Alex knew the gun, having once seen it demonstrated at a police arms exhibit in New York. It was generally considered the most efficient small automatic weapon in the world.

Behind Fast could be made out the figures of others.

He strode into the room, his fox-face grinning and came forward a dozen steps. At his side was Fay Morgan, her visage in high triumph and hate. Behind her came Bill and Martha and two efficient looking strangers. All four wore combat dungarees, all four carried Uzi submachine guns and from their shoulders and belts hung canvas bags of the type usually utilized for spare ammunition and grenades, both fragmentation and gas.

Fay Morgan alone wore no gas mask. Her dark Welsh eyes were blazing and although her words were for all, her gaze was directly on Alex Germain as she shrilled, "You all laughed at me! You all were contemptuous of me, rejected me! All except Jack. But now you'll take your medicine! Now you'll crawl! While Jack and I will go on forever."

Behind the two of them, the other four deployed, spread out across the room.

The enclave members, on their feet, spilling their

folding chairs, in complete confusion stumbled in retreat toward the podium at the far end of the hall. Alex jumped down from the stand and stood next to Lilith, his eyes darting about the room. There was no exit, save for the door through which the killers had entered.

Jack Fast was vaingloriously juvenile enough to gloat. He called to Alex, "Didn't know I was onto you, did you, my stupid friend? It so happens, I checked with the Chief and he made it clear you weren't on our team."

His eyes went around to the rest of the confused—some mewling, some crying, some stifling small screams—assembly. "And you were all taken in by the Beaumonts retiring early because of supposedly being drunk. And that I was off the scene, making out with Fay. You didn't know Fay was one of the first to be told of this meeting and immediately tipped me off."

Cohen called out from the podium. "Can't we talk about this?"

Fast laughed in obvious enjoyment. "So far as I'm concerned, you can talk until your last minute, you kike. All right, all right, everybody down to the far end of the room."

He came forward a few more steps, threatening with his gun, Fay triumphantly at his side.

Alex took Lilith by the arm and began to work his way down the room, along the side nearest the patio. The dog padded along behind.

Lilith protested fearfully, trying to get her arm away from him. "What ... what ..." She was obviously as terrified as any of the others.

Suddenly, Jack Fast reached his right hand out,

holding the submachine gun solely by its pistol grip and shoved Fay brutally forward.

"You get in there with the rest of them, you fuck-crazy whore!" he laughed.

She sprawled forward a dozen steps before coming to her knees. She turned, her eyes bugging in astonishment. "Jack ... Jack ... darling!" she screamed. "What do you mean!"

He laughed again, a high neurotic squeal, no humor there. "The orders from above are you all go, baby. No exceptions."

He hadn't seen Martha come up behind him.

She brought up a foot into the small of his back and sent him bowling forward after Fay, reeling in the attempt to keep his balance.

"Those are the orders, all right, Jack," she said flatly. "All of you go. The Chief says no exceptions."

He staggered erect. And though his face was masked, obviously he was staring. "Why, you bitch!" he screamed. "I'm running things here!" In his rage he brought up the Uzi gun and aimed.

One of the stocky gunmen, the newcomers on the scene, called out, "Sorry. No firing pin in the gun we gave you, Jack. Tough shit."

Martha's gun chopped out a short burst and Jack Fast unbelieving to the last, crumbled forward, the useless submachine gun dropping to the floor.

"Okay," Martha rasped over her shoulder. "The gas first, boys."

Alex had sidled behind Lilith to hide his movements. His hand darted toward his belt. His motions went undetected in the utter confusion that permeated the conference room.

His throw was perfect. Martha Beaumont staggered backward, her eyes bugging behind the mask lenses, as the knife buried itself in her stomach.

In the next ten seconds the confusion dissolved into chaos, into bedlam.

Alex snapped, "Get 'em, boy," and Buda was darting forward, running low, his mouth wide, slavering, his huge fighting teeth bared.

Alex hadn't noticed Hsu Fu coming along behind him as he had pressed up to the fore of the room, but now he heard his Kiai shout, "SUT!"

The guns of Nick, Gino and Bill Beaumont were swinging in attempt to track the heavy-set war dog. But the fast moving Buda was working with an advantage. Chairs were every which way, some fallen, some still standing. He darted among them as he advanced, somewhat like a broken field football quarterback.

A burst went off, completely missing the Vizsla, splattering on the floor and ricocheting, some of the slugs to find home in the screaming mass of humanity pressing back in desperate effort to find escape that didn't exist.

But the burst hadn't come from Buda's immediate quarry. He was zeroed in on one of the hitmen, Nick or Gino.

There is often something in the most experienced combat man when faced with a fighting dog, if he has never been checked out on such and few have. Perhaps it is an instinct when man faces slavering teeth, a fearful instinct come down from the infancy of the race. Or perhaps it was that Gino Bova had been savaged by a dog while still a child. Whatever, instead of trying to bring his gun to bear, he attempted to step quickly backward, holding the weapon up as a shield to ward the raging animal off. And then, one hand went to his throat for protection.

But Buda did not go for the throat. Three thousand years of war dog training of his ancestors on the part of the Huns was behind him. He slashed for the groin, slashed, sunk teeth and ripped. And then he was sliding away at unbelievable fighting dog speed.

Gino's scream echoed from the ceiling, from the walls.

Bill Beaumont had dashed forward to Martha, who was staggering, her goggled eyes staring down at the heavy knife, buried to the hilt in her belly.

Alex swung Lilith before him and backed quickly. He threw one of the drapes to the side and lunged heavily backward into the picture window that opened onto the patio, hauling Lilith behind him. Even as he crashed on through the heavy glass he saw two more things. A gas bomb exploded at the far end of the room, vomiting green fumes. And at the door he could see a staggering Marcelo, coughing blood, enter the door and fumble for the light switch.

Even as they landed on the flagstones of the patio amidst a thousand brutally sharp glass shards, the lights went out, a gun chattered hysterically, and Alex, fighting desperately to keep from passing out, could hear Hsu Fu's Kiai shout again, "SUT!"

He hauled Lilith to her feet, reeling himself.

"You all right?" he panted. He was a bloody mess, an untold number of cuts having shredded clothes, back, arms, legs and head.

She was as stumbling as he and unable to answer.

"Quick," he blurted. "The kitchen." He began lurching in that direction.

The kitchen was dark. He fumbled. "The lights," he panted to Lilith.

Somehow she got them on.

He took up a meat cleaver from the butcher's block and a heavy slicing knife which he forced into her hands.

"Come on," he said. He was almost completely blinded from blood seeping into his eyes from cuts on his head and forehead. He didn't know if she was following or not.

He stumbled forward to the heavy door leading into the conference room. But even as he approached it, the nearly two hundred members of the enclave began surging out, screaming, shouting terror, yelling ultimate fear, pushing, shoving each other. Some were on their hands and knees crawling for the open. It was each for himself.

Alex couldn't have made his way through them even had he been without wounds. He collapsed to the ground but even before the blackness washed in he realized what had happened. When Marcelo had thrown the switch and the lights went out, there were some 190 terrified community members milling about, out of their minds with fear. And there were but two or at most three of the gunmen on their feet and capable of action. They were not enough in the face of Buda, the kenpo practicing Chinaman and nearly two hundred frantic, wild, would-be escapees. Bill Beaumont and Nick Terry must have been trampled into unconsciousness in the stampede for the door.

Aftermath

When he awakened, the pink flushes of Mexican dawn, unrivaled in North America, were coming through the windows. He was in his bed. He was a mass of bandages. Around the bed were Lilith, Ursula and a white smocked enclave member. On the foot of the bed, his right leg forward in a splint and his right ear heavily bandaged was Buda. They were all, including the Vizsla—nay, especially the dog—looking at him worriedly.

Alex Germain got out, "It must have been something I ate."

Ursula snorted. "Kind of impetuous, aren't you? Jumping through that window really got things rolling."

Lilith sat next to him on the edge of the bed and touched long fingers to his face. "Darling, are you all right?"

"That's a good question." He looked down at his heavily bandaged arms. "It wouldn't seem so."

The smocked man said, "I'm Doctor Walexca. Most of your cuts are superficial. However, I haven't practiced medicine since the Franco-Prussian War in 1871. You should immediately see a more competent practitioner. You can claim to have been in an automobile accident."

"I know one in Celaya," Lilith said quickly.

Ursula narrowed her Germanic blue eyes. "You can trust him? Alex might have to hide out for a week or more and Celaya is awfully near."

"We're very fond of each other," Lilith said lowly, and averting her eyes from her lover. "A few years ago we occasionally slept with each other. He's married now but we're still close friends."

Alex switched subject. "What happened?"

Ursula said, after breathing deeply, "You saw most of it before you blacked out. Seven of us are dead, including Marcelo, who Fast and the others had evidently left as finished off, back in the entrada to the hotel. He had more life in him than they suspected. He made it through to turn out the lights. David and Hsu Fu are dead. I don't think either of them really wished to live on, given the end of the enclave. They led the attack, if you could call it that. Several more are hurt to various degrees, hurts that were largely afflicted in the crush. All of the gunmen are dead, the final three kicked and battered with chairs until they were bloody messes."

Alex looked at the former doctor. "Are you going to be able to dispose of . . ."

Walexca was nodding. "Yes, we have ample time now. Ursula will post a notice on the hotel door that it is closed and will pay off and dismiss all the help so that no outsiders will enter. The gunfire could not have been heard. The conference room was soundproof. Except for a handful of us, needed to get rid of all evidence, the community will disperse today, going by car to Celaya and Queretero. The cars will ferry back and forth carrying four or five at a time."

Ursula said urgently, "Alex, the problem is this. How are we all going to keep in touch, without Somerlott's gang ferreting us out? We've got to work in concert and, eventually, of course, get back together again."

He had already worked that out the day before. He said, "Listen, carefully. We're going to have to utilize the old cell system. It's been used by anarchists, nihilists and other undergrounds for centuries. Each cell has five members who know each other and how to get in touch with each other. But none of them know the location of any others, except for their leader. He knows two other cell leaders. In case any cell member is caught, he can betray only the other four cell members. If the cell leader is caught, and he must not be if at all possible, he must be dedicated enough to be ready to suicide. If he is caught, he is in a position to betray not only his own cell members but the other two cell leaders he knows, if he is tortured or subjected to truth serum. Each cell leader will be in touch with one of a central committee of three, which I suppose is up to the vote, but I suggest that it consist of you, Nuscha, Lilith and myself. The committee will be our central authority—subject of course to the vote of the full membership. The system is obviously not fool proof but it is the best devised that I know of."

The doctor looked at Ursula. "We'd better get down to the others and arrange this cell system before any of them start out of town."

"Yes, of course." Ursula turned and headed for the door, after bending a wistful eye at Alex and an envious one at Lilith.

When the others were gone, Alex looked at the woman he loved.

He said emptily, "We've won round one, Lilith."

She nodded. "Yes, but there will be other rounds. The fight has just begun."

The End